"What's The Problem?"

"I stuck my keys in my back pocket." Cecilia bent over to unload her arms.

"Allow me." She felt Jeff's fingers inching into her pocket.

"I found them." Slowly, his hand slipped out of her pocket, and the keys jangled softly. "Do you remember painting 'Just Married' on my car the night of my senior prom?"

"I'm not sure I want to admit it," she muttered.

"My date thought *I* did it . . . as a proposal."

"You're kidding." She unlocked the door, her heart beating an erratic tattoo. "Really, Jeff, do we have to rehash all this ancient history?"

He patiently unloaded the packages she held in her arms, dropping the bags to the floor. "I've just been thinking. You chased me so hard for so long." He grinned lazily. "I think it's time you caught me."

Dear Reader:

I hope you've been enjoying 1989, our "Year of the Man" at Silhouette Desire. Every one of the twelve authors who are contributing a *Man of the Month* has created a very special someone for your reading pleasure. Each man is unique, and each author's style, plot and characterization give you a different insight into her man's story.

From January to December, 1989 will be a twelve-month extravaganza, spotlighting one book each month with special cover treatment as a tribute to the Silhouette Desire hero—our *Man of the Month*!

You'll find these men who've been created by your favorite authors irresistible. Naomi Horton's Slater McCall is indeed *A Dangerous Kind of Man*, coming this April, and love, betrayal, greed and revenge are all part of Lucy Gordon's dramatic *Vengeance Is Mine*, featuring Luke Harmon as Mr. May.

Don't let these men get away!

Yours,

Isabel Swift
Senior Editor & Editorial Coordinator

PATRICIA BURROUGHS
Beguiled Again

Silhouette Desire

Published by Silhouette Books New York

America's Publisher of Contemporary Romance

SILHOUETTE BOOKS
300 East 42nd St., New York, N.Y. 10017

ISBN: 0-373-05490-4

First Silhouette Books printing April 1989

Printed in the U.S.A.

Books by Patricia Burroughs

Silhouette Desire

Razzmatazz #477
Beguiled Again #490

PATRICIA BURROUGHS,

the mother of three, learned the hard way that the only way to survive day-to-day life in a chaotic household is with lots of patience and laughter. Before she became a published writer, her activities included being a Cub Scout den leader, a preschool teacher and a P.T.A. volunteer. Thus she accomplished much of her "research" for the children in *Beguiled Again* long before she conceived the idea for the book. However, she firmly believes that her fictitious children live and breathe because of the inspiration of her real children: Douglas (who is not Peter), James (who is not Brad) and Scott—who most definitely isn't Anne-Elizabeth!

To Carol Budd and Maria Greene,
whose friendly bayonets always knew
when and how hard to nudge.

And to Carol Jerina.
It's all your fault!

One

It couldn't be him.

Cecilia's heart pounded as she plastered herself against a toy rack and counted to ten. That man—the one who had whizzed past the toy aisle with only a cursory glance in her direction—couldn't be who she thought he was.

Cecilia edged to the end of the aisle and peeked around the corner just in time to see him again. His profile was clear and sharp as he hesitated at the head of the third aisle down. Her heart leaped into her throat.

It couldn't be him—but it was.

It was definitely Jefferson Smith, all six feet of him, standing fifteen strides away from her, impeccably dressed in a charcoal gray suit that bespoke the success their high school yearbook had predicted for him. Jefferson Smith, most likely to succeed—most likely to cause heart failure to one Cecilia Greene Evans all these years later.

Cecilia retreated to the relative safety of the toy aisle, one hand clutching the stretched neck of her Dallas Maverick sweatshirt, the other clutching her stomach. She felt weak, sicker than before.

She turned toward her four-year-old and her already roiling stomach plummeted. "Anne-Elizabeth!" she gasped.

Her overall-clad daughter was scaling the shelves, balancing precariously as she groped for the top shelf. "I want finger paints," Anne-Elizabeth announced loudly.

Cecilia darted across the aisle, snatched the straps of the child's overalls and lifted her to the floor. "We've got to go home," Cecilia whispered. "Now."

"I know. Mommy's sick." Anne-Elizabeth stared at her solemnly, then pointed upward. "I want finger paints."

"Over my dead—" Cecilia began.

"You pwomised!" Anne-Elizabeth folded her plump arms across her stomach, her glare mutinous. Then her eyes grew limpid, her woeful expression calculated to break a mother's heart. "Pwease, Mommy? Pwease get me the paints."

Cecilia squeezed her burning eyes closed and swallowed hard. All she had needed from the grocery store was two pizzas, and look where that had gotten her. Yes, in a weak moment she had promised a toy—but not finger paints to smear from baseboards to ceilings. But now, right this very minute, Jefferson Smith was three aisles away. She'd do anything to escape the grocery store without running into him.

Not about to scale the shelves herself, she swatted at the box, trying to knock it askew so she could grasp the lower corner. Instead, when her fingertips grazed its bottom edge, the box fell forward and crashed to the floor. Anne-Elizabeth gleefully grabbed the paints. Cecilia hoped two things: one, that Jefferson Smith didn't round the corner to investigate the commotion; two, that the paint jars were plastic.

"Come on, sweetheart," she hissed, and grabbed her daughter by the fleshy part of her upper arms and hoisted her into the basket. Cecilia propelled the cart in the opposite direction from Jefferson Smith as fast as her trembling knees allowed.

Then she tripped over a loose shoelace, stumbled and caught herself on the cart. Damn and blast and God bless America.

"Oops," Anne-Elizabeth said, peering over the side of the basket at her mother's dirty sneakers. "Can I tie 'em?"

"Later, sweetheart," Cecilia said sweetly through her teeth. She glanced over her shoulder, then grabbed two pepperoni deluxe pizzas that weren't even on sale from the end of the frozen food aisle.

She rolled the basket into the checkout line farthest from the express lane, her heart pumping hard and temples throbbing. She felt sick, grimy and cornered. Why the heck was Jefferson Smith in *her* grocery store, wearing an Italian suit on a day when she wasn't wearing a speck of make-up? After all these years . . . She hadn't realized he lived in Dallas anymore. And her hair! She reached instinctively for her hair, a frizzy halo similar to her daughter's tousled red curls. Neither had received the benefit of comb or brush or mirror since morning.

"Walph needs dog food and I want candy." Anne-Elizabeth swung a leg over the side of the basket and climbed out. Cecilia was too tired, too achy, to argue. Besides, she was darn grateful her daughter had reminded her of the dog food. She wasn't up to another trip.

Anne-Elizabeth grabbed a chocolate bar and sauntered toward a display of play balls at the end of the coffee aisle. Cecilia scanned what she could see of the store. As long as Anne-Elizabeth stayed in sight it was simpler to let her wander than to fight with her.

Just let me get out of here without facing Jefferson Smith, she pleaded silently to whatever twisted fates had doomed her to such a disaster. The last thing in the world she needed or wanted was to cross paths with that arrogant jerk!

As he clutched a small can of decaffeinated coffee, Jeff glanced at his watch and grimaced. April 15 was exactly one month away. With Kathy on maternity leave, he'd work past ten again tonight. How could an accountant as careful, as meticulous as Kathy schedule a baby at tax time? His frustration mounted as he studied the coffee display and decided to hell with it.

He replaced the can and snatched a foil bag from the shelf, dumped its coffee beans into the self-serve grinder and flipped the switch. The grinder whirred, the bag filled, and the aroma of heavy-duty, industrial-strength, keep-your-eyes-open-till-midnight Colombian coffee filled the air. Just the smell of it was enough to wake him up.

"That thing's noisy."

He stopped in the midst of detaching the bag from the grinder and glanced toward the tiny girl watching him from the end of the aisle, her large green eyes wide and accusing.

"My mommy doesn't get that kind."

Jeff stared down at the urchin, at her tangled mop of red hair, her purple T-shirt, her faded overalls and her ridiculous red high-topped sneakers with purple shoelaces. "I...I beg your pardon?" he asked.

"My mommy says that kind's too 'spensive." The child's full lips clamped into a stubborn, chocolate-smeared line.

"Well," Jeff said sternly. "Your mother is welcome to her opinion, but I'm sure that I—"

Suddenly a hand reached around the corner, grabbed the straps of the child's overalls and yanked her out of his sight.

"But Mommy..." He heard the little girl's fading wail.

Jeff forced his attention back to the coffee, frowning. He meticulously folded the top of the bag over three times. His curiosity getting the better of him, he walked to the front of the store to see if he child was safely contained. Her loud protests were easy to follow as she was herded through the automatic doors. His gaze swung from the child to her mother and froze. The woman bore a startling resemblance to—

No. It must be someone who looked like her, that's all. Her blazing hair was the same, but many women had such hair. The oversize sweatshirt and tight jeans fit the image of the teenager she had been the last time he had seen her, but after all, that was seventeen years ago. It was a coincidence, nothing more, he told himself firmly.

But he didn't listen to himself. He hurried to the front door and squinted through the glass as the woman and the child climbed into a red Suburban. It was hard to tell from this distance, and a misting rain was falling, as well, but damned if she didn't look like...Cecil.

Just the thought of Cecilia Greene made him take a couple of steps backward. Had she seen him? The door whooshed closed in front of him and he clutched the coffee in a white-knuckled grip. Cecilia Greene, the albatross around his neck, the perpetual-motion dynamo who had made his life a living hell his last year in high school. His stomach burned.

He plowed his fingers through his hair, torn between curiosity and trepidation. No, it wouldn't be her after all these years. Just a coincidence, he told himself again, returning to the express checkout. The last person in the world he wanted to see was Cecilia Greene.

There were only two people ahead of him, so in minutes he was headed through the automatic doors with his coffee. As he walked toward his car he passed the empty space where the red Suburban had been. A peacock blue wallet beckoned from a shallow puddle of water.

The tension crawled down his neck and spine. His instinct of self-preservation warned him to leave it alone. Instead he stooped and retrieved the dripping wallet. He was being ridiculous. That frazzled woman with the untidy tot couldn't possibly be the hoydenish Cecilia Greene.

He opened the wallet, saw the name imprinted on the checks inside and groaned.

Cecilia drove into her neighborhood and waited for the surge of relief to sweep over her. But her chest kept pounding and her racing pulse refused to slow. She couldn't believe that after all these years the sight of Jeff could still shake her up. "I think I have the flu," she rationalized aloud.

"Look!" Anne-Elizabeth's shrill voice pierced through the fog of Cecilia's reverie. "It's a po-weece car!"

Cecilia glanced at the flashing red lights in her rearview mirror. "Oh, no." She checked the speedometer; she wasn't even speeding.

"What the heck is it now?" She pulled over, rolled down the window and waited for the police officer. She was almost home. Why did this have to happen? And why today?

"May I see your driver's license, please?"

"Yes, Officer, I've got it right here . . . somewhere." The officer looked too young for a driver's license himself, much less old enough to be demanding hers. She rummaged through her purse. Her hand emerged empty. "Uh, why did you pull me over?"

"You didn't use your left turn signal at the corner, ma'am," he replied courteously.

"I always use my turn indicator, Officer. Excuse me." She flipped on the blinker and got out of the car, slamming the door behind her. "Stay right where you are, kiddo," she snapped over her shoulder.

Seeing the officer's astounded expression, she shook her head. "Not you, Officer." She pointed at Anne-Elizabeth, poised and ready to climb out the rear window. "Her!"

Circling the car, she stood and stared at the taillight that failed to flash. "Damnation."

"Sorry, but I'm going to have to give you a citation, ma'am. May I see your driver's license, now?"

"Yeah, sure. Let me find it for you." Climbing back into the Suburban, she searched the brown grocery bag—with no success.

Anne-Elizabeth hung out the back window. "Are you gonna take Mommy to jail?"

"No, darlin'. Just writing her a ticket." The officer tipped his visored hat back on his head and stepped closer to the rear window. "How old are you?"

Keep talking, Annie, Cecilia thought. Just give me a little more time. She knew she could count on her daughter to keep the officer occupied while she groped under the seats for her wallet.

"I'm Anne-Ewizabeth and I'm four years old and I can spell my name. *A-N-N-E* hyphen *E-L-I-Z-A-B-E-T-H*," she rattled off in a singsong voice. "Is that a weal gun? Does it have bullets in it?"

"Don't worry." The officer patted his holster. "It won't hurt you."

"Wet me shoot it!" Anne-Elizabeth lunged forward, her plump, sticky hand outstretched.

"Hey, wait a minute!"

The officer jumped and surveyed the hand smear on his shirt. "Look, lady," he said, irritation in his voice. "I need that license now, if you don't mind!"

"Of course I don't mind," Cecilia said. "But I can't find it! I wrote a check at the supermarket. I must have left my wallet there!"

Frowning, he pulled out his pad and flipped it open. "Name?"

Cecilia groaned. Out of the corner of her eye, she saw a small red convertible stop behind them. Dazed, amazed and flabbergasted, she watched Jefferson Smith unwind his lanky frame from the car. What in blazes—

Her mouth fell open when she saw her blue wallet in Jefferson Smith's hand. This wasn't real. This wasn't happening to her. This was a nightmare.

"Cecil?" He peered in the window at her. "It really is you. Imagine that, after all these years."

"Where did you get that?" she asked breathlessly.

"I found it in the parking lot in a puddle." He lifted the soggy wallet.

"Why... thank you, Jeff." She took it from him, overwhelmed with conflicting emotions. Jeff stepped aside, and Cecilia restrained her temper and accepted her ticket gracefully.

"Bye-bye," Anne-Elizabeth sang as the officer pulled away.

Jeff took a step closer to the Suburban and peered inside. He grinned, damn him, and her heart catapulted into her throat.

"Some things don't change do they, Cecil? You still can't drive a mile without getting yourself in trouble."

"Thanks for bringing my wallet," Cecilia said.

Jeff's eyebrows drew together, "I'm really sorry about your ticket."

"Mommy, the pizzas aren't cold anymore. Can I eat 'em?" Anne-Elizabeth ripped the box half-open.

Cecilia wrenched it from her hands. "No, they're still raw. Just sit down. We're leaving." She buckled her daughter securely into the seat, then faced Jeff, her pretense at civility wearing thin. "Don't worry about the ticket, Jeff. I can handle everything without any further assistance from you."

Jeff interrupted her with a shake of his head. "I don't think so, Cecil. I happened to notice the balance in your checkbook."

"You *what*?"

"I know how it seems—but I wasn't being nosy. I was looking for your name and address and your wallet fell open to your check register."

"How dare you!"

"Calm down, Cecil." His hand closed over hers, his palm surprisingly cool and smooth. "I'm not prying, honest. But you really do need to do something about that checkbook. It's a mess."

She tugged her hand away from him. "For your information, Mr. Smith," she hissed, "there's a perfectly good explanation for my checkbook, but it happens to be none of your damn business!"

"Hey, I'm sorry, kid," he protested, looking genuinely chagrined.

"I'm not a kid, Jeff!"

"No, you're certainly not. You've changed." He studied her intently.

She felt her face flush. "Most people do change between the ages of fourteen and thirty-two."

"Who would have thought..." Jeff murmured, his voice velvety and soft and all too pleasing to her ears.

"Thought what?" she asked breathlessly.

"You..." He angled his head and narrowed his eyes. "You're pretty pale. You really look ill, Cecilia."

Cecilia gritted her teeth, squeezed her eyes closed and wished for a gun to shoot him and an open hole to bury him in. "I thank you very much for your concern. No, I'm not well. I'm sick. I'm coming down with the flu. Goodbye, Jeff."

Jeff glanced at his watch. "I'm already late for a meeting, but I'd better follow you. You don't look like you're going to make it." He strode toward his car.

Why was he doing this? Cecilia wondered. But with a weary ache numbing every joint in her body, she had no more energy to argue. She pulled away from the curb and slowly drove the short distance home.

What the hell was he doing? Jeff wondered as he followed the Suburban down the shady street of aging brick homes that had been his old neighborhood. He hadn't been here or thought of Cecilia Greene in years, and here he was, playing Sir Galahad to her maiden-in-distress act. The cool wind whipping through his hair did little to explain the way his blood was racing, probably from out-and-out madness.

Her checks had been embossed "Cecilia Evans." Evans...Evans. He vaguely remembered Robert Evans, remembered hearing that they'd married.

He parked on the street as Cecilia swerved into her daffodil-lined driveway too quickly. She cut the corner short, crushing a row of yellow blooms with her front right tire. The house seemed oddly unperturbed by its near brush with destruction. But, then, he thought wryly, that old house had probably gotten used to her erratic ways. From its L-shaped porch that wrapped its southwest corner, to its irregular native red stone exterior that dripped ivy from almost every surface, to its diamond-paned windows, the house seemed a buxom old dowager, ready to absorb Cecilia into its protective embrace.

In front of the house, a pair of spreading pecan trees cast the yard in shadow. Purple violets filled the flower beds beneath the trees, and a rusty wagon lay overturned amid the violets. The homey scene was marred only by a plastic Uzi machine gun propped against the wagon. There was probably a metaphor there, if he cared to pursue it. He didn't.

He strode toward the Suburban as her car door opened, and offered his hand. She ignored him and fumbled with the grocery sack, instead.

"You get the kid and I'll get the dog food," he told her firmly, spying the large bag in the back of the vehicle.

"You don't have to do this." She reached across the sack to unbuckle her little girl.

"And who is going to carry in fifty pounds of dog food if I don't? You?"

Her head snapped back and she faced him with sparks of green fire shooting from her eyes. "Who the heck do you think usually does it—elves?" She paled, and he reached involuntarily for her shoulder, stopping just short of touching her. "I don't know why you're doing this, or what you're trying to prove."

Her voice was just as he remembered, a little husky in a pleasing sort of way. Now why had he noticed that? "Cecil." Jeff jerked his hand back and spoke more gruffly then he intended. "Calm down. Okay?" He softened his words with a quirky grin. "I just want to help. Give me a break, huh?"

He heaved the dog food onto his shoulder and stood waiting for her as the child scrambled out of the car and scurried up the sloping yard to the house, shouting at the top of her lungs, "Mommy bwung home a man!"

He read Cecilia's chagrin in the straight line of her back and the rigidity of her shoulders. But even her anger and frustration didn't still the gentle sway of her hips as she followed her daughter up the cracked cement walkway. Jeff followed, not even bothering to avert his gaze. She hadn't grown an inch, and certainly hadn't picked up much extra weight. But what was there was . . . softer, maybe.

Damn. He yanked his gaze away in time to see another youngster come bounding down the porch steps. "A man? Where?" the boy demanded. Crunching into a carrot, he stared at Jeff, then dropped a soccer ball and trapped it under the toe of his sneaker.

Jeff was rather taken aback. Two children.

"You're home early," Cecilia told the boy, brushing his red hair out of his eyes as she passed him.

"Friday's an early release day, remember?" The boy pointed the chewed end of his carrot at Jeff. "Who's he?"

"Just an old friend. Jeff, this is Brad. Brad, this is Jeff," she mumbled as she climbed the steps.

The kid stood in front of Jeff and bounced the ball from one foot to the other, then off his knees and to his feet again. "I did it seventeen times without missing," he boasted, never missing a beat of his juggling.

Cecilia stopped in the doorway and called, "Brad, move out of the way."

The ball glanced off Brad's toe and soared toward the street. "You messed me up," he complained, taking off after it.

Balancing the large bag of dog food on his shoulder, Jeff paused in the doorway. His dark brows met in a scowl. Cars, space figures and baseball cards littered the floor, a veritable mine field of boyish booby traps. As he stepped carefully across the foyer floor, his gaze was drawn into the living room, with its overstuffed chintz chairs, a love seat and more clutter.

Then he saw the fireplace. A brass antelope nestled on the hearth, and behind it, a profusion of large silk butterflies hung in the white-enameled firebox. Somehow, butterflies in Cecilia's fireplace seemed whimsically appropriate.

He stepped forward and something crunched beneath his shoe. "Damn!" He kicked aside a small plastic car and moved on into the den. A guy could break his leg walking through this disaster.

Cecilia stood facing a tall, thin blond boy in glasses.

"Mom, how could you?" The boy waved an envelope in his mother's face. "You bounced three checks. Three! I told you to let me balance the checkbook last week, but oh, no! You didn't have time! And now—"

"Peter," Cecilia ground out through clenched teeth. "This is not the time for this discussion. If you want the checkbook, take it!" She slapped it into his outstretched palm. "Balance it or burn it—just get it out of my sight!" Without giving him a chance to respond, she walked into the kitchen area.

Peter turned and saw Jeff, his eyes widening in surprise. He stiffened, then left the room, muttering under his breath.

"Charming child," Jeff remarked, more grateful than ever for his bachelorhood. Three? She and Robert had three children?

She spun toward him, her pale cheeks suffusing with color. "Just drop the dog food where you are. I'll have the boys take it out later."

Jeff warily did as she commanded. "Are you all right?"

"Yeah," she answered weakly. "I just need to sit down for a minute." She dropped into a chair at the breakfast table and put her head in her hands.

He needed to leave. He wanted to leave. Jeff slid his hands in his pockets and glanced uncertainly around the large kitchen-den combination. An assortment of trophies decorated the bay windowsill, and a soccer ball fought for space on the cluttered surface of a rolltop desk. Jutting from under the brown leather couch was the rump of a quivering beast, most probably a Great Dane.

"Cecil," he asked tentatively, "is something wrong with your dog?"

She raised her head. "He's terrified of strangers. If he hides his head, he thinks you can't see him."

"Mmm..." Jeff cast a wary eye at the dog's angular derriere.

Three sharp knocks shook the back door and another boy entered the the room. Jeff did a double take. Son of a gun, not four!

"Mikey, would you please get me a glass of ice water?" She buried her face in her hands again.

"Sure thing, Mrs. Evans." The dark-haired boy sauntered confidently across the kitchen and jammed a glass under the dispenser in the refrigerator door.

"Well, since everything seems to be under control..." Jeff began.

"Mom needs her scissors," the boy said, thrusting the glass at Cecilia. "That's why I'm here."

"I don't know where they are. How soon does she need them?" She took the glass with one hand; the other never left her forehead.

"She needs 'em right now, but don't worry, I'll find 'em." He dashed to the back door and opened it. "Hey, Vincent! Come 'ere and help me find the scissors!" A younger dark-haired boy joined him, and they raced into the living room, shouting for Brad and Peter.

Jeff shifted uneasily. Cecilia seemed to have forgotten him. This whole scene reminded him of Cub Scout day camp. All that was lacking was the chiggers. He cleared his throat.

She stared blankly in his direction. "I'm sorry..."

"Are you sure you're—" He was no more than halfway finished, when she began to slump. With a startled oath, Jeff dashed across the room and caught her just before she hit the table. Her body slid against his, and he felt her feverish skin. With one arm under her shoulder and the other grasping her free arm, he held her in an impossible position for lifting. He uttered a sharp curse and dragged her toward the sofa.

Halfway there, he was suddenly confronted with what appeared to be at least one hundred forty pounds of snarling Ralph. "Wait a minute, dog," he pleaded, easing Cecilia's limp body to the floor and putting himself between her and the dog. Of all times for the mangy cur to discover he had guts.

"What are you doin' to my mommy?" Anne-Elizabeth leaped at Jeff, and he thought he heard the child growl. Then a set of teeth, obviously not canine, closed on his wrist. Jeff gave a yelp and jerked his hand free. The mophaired child fell backward, screaming bloody murder. But before Jeff could inspect the damage, the snarling dog and Anne-Elizabeth's angry wails had summoned the boys out of the woodwork.

"What'd you do to my sister?" Brad demanded.

"Look what he did to your mom!" Mikey shouted.

They all sprang at Jeff at once.

"Oh, hell!" Jeff ducked his head and threw himself across Cecilia's limp body in an effort to protect her from the onslaught.

A piercing whistle split the air, ceasing all movements. Jeff raised his head and saw Peter standing in the doorway.

"What's going on here?" Peter's blue-gray eyes scanned the room with clear disapproval as he twirled a shiny referee's whistle.

Jeff leaped up. "Help me. Your mom fainted."

"What did you do to her?" Peter exclaimed, running to his mother's side. "Look, buddy," Jeff growled, "I didn't do anything. She's sick, can't you tell? Now shut up and help me get her to the sofa." Cecilia moaned in his arms, and he felt a strange protective sensation stir within him.

Jeff placed Cecilia gently on the sofa after Peter cleared newspapers and a basket of clean laundry out of the way. Jeff shot his hand out in time to save Cecilia from being doused with ice water. "Mikey, I don't know who in the heck you are, but if you throw a drop of water on this lady, you're history!"

Mikey backed off, his eyes wide. "Come on, Vinny, I think we'd better go get Mom!" They disappeared.

"Where's your dad?" Jeff asked Peter.

The boy's faced shuttered over.

It was his sister who responded. "With Monica."

"Monica?" Jeff echoed. "You have another sister?"

"No, dummy," Brad chimed in. "He married her."

"He mawwied her," Anne-Elizabeth repeated.

Peter stared belligerently at him.

What now? Jeff stared helplessly at Cecilia's pale face as Peter bustled around in the kitchen, then returned to his mother's side. Her eyes finally fluttered open, and Jeff felt relief flow through him. She opened her mouth to speak, but Peter thrust a thermometer in. She blinked from Peter to Jeff, to Peter again in apparent confusion, then closed her eyes once more.

Jeff studied his watch and anxiously counted off the minutes, casting surreptitious glances at Cecilia. But when he reached for the thermometer, Peter snatched it away and carried it to the window to read. "Mom, you've got a hundred and one. You're sick."

Brad whirled toward Jeff. "That means you've gotta get outa here, mister. Mom doesn't allow company when we've got fever."

Jeff started to tell the kid exactly what he thought of him, but was interrupted by a very welcome adult voice.

"What seems to be the problem?" A tall woman with dark almond eyes surveyed the scene from the open back door, flanked by Mikey and Vinny. She cast her appraising look at Jeff. "I don't believe we've met?"

"Jefferson Smith." He offered his hand awkwardly, feeling uncharacteristically ill at ease under her close scrutiny.

"Carol Bellini," she responded with a slight smile. "Are you a friend of Cecilia's?"

"In a manner of speaking, yes. We, er, go back a long way."

"Mmm-hmm." She crossed toward Cecilia, patting Ralph's head as she passed him. The disgusting mutt wiggled with delight.

"Carol . . ." Cecilia croaked. "What's happening?"

"That man hurt you, Mommy. But me and Walph stopped him." Anne-Elizabeth beamed with pride.

"I did not . . ." Jeff began.

"And he twied to hit me, but I'm too stwong," Anne-Elizabeth continued.

"I did not!" Jeff said desperately, but the clamoring of the children as each babbled a different version of the fracas drowned out his voice. He closed his eyes in despair. Damn, nothing had changed. Chaos still surrounded Cecilia.

His suit was rumpled and covered with dog hairs, and he'd already missed a meeting. Did he have time to go home and change before his next appointment? First he had to get out of this madhouse. Then maybe the world would shift back to normality.

But when he glanced at Cecilia's pale face surrounded by the anxious faces of her children, he felt a pang of . . . of what? What was it about her that grabbed hold of him, made him feel so protective? Those same waifish eyes, that same fiery mop of hair, that same full, pouting lower lip . . . No doubt about it, she'd turned out better than he had ever suspected a skinny fourteen-year-old possibly could. But what he was responding to was something else.

He couldn't explain the smile tugging at his lips, the amusement suddenly bubbling up inside him at the sight of her, the thought of her, the reality of Cecilia Greene crashing back into his life again, after all these years. He should be gnashing his teeth with frustration. Instead he was grinning like an idiot.

What the heck had come over him? Whatever it was, he'd better get control of it fast. Without a word, he slipped out of the room.

Ten minutes in this household was enough to convince him he didn't have the time, energy or fortitude for any further dealings with Cecilia Greene.

Two

————

Disjointed thoughts rattled in Cecilia's head. Jeff had hit Anne-Elizabeth? Maybe Anne-Elizabeth had hit Jeff. Now *that* made sense.

Unless he had been a dream... But no. If there was one thing she was sure of, Jeff Smith was real. Even now she could close her eyes and see that oh-so-familiar, yet totally alien face staring at her, sable brows arching wryly as he shook his head.

Swept away in the undertow of fever and humiliation, she'd been too ill to care when he left. She levered herself up on one elbow and tried to read the wall clock in the kitchen. Peter came through the room with his toothbrush and pillow under his arm.

"I'm sorry I was such a pest, Mom." He ducked his blond head and dug the toe of his Converse high-tops into the carpet. "I balanced the checkbook for you. We're staying at Carol's tonight." He stooped awkwardly and pecked her on the cheek.

"Peter," she croaked, fighting to keep her eyes open. "What happened to Jeff?"

His thin shoulders stiffened and his chin thrust forward. "Don't worry about him, Mom. He's a jerk."

"I know," she muttered hoarsely, sinking back into the cushions. "How well I remember."

An hour later, Cecilia struggled out of a restless sleep and walked on shaky legs down the hall to the bathroom. She squinted at her watch; it was seven-thirty.

She washed her face. The aspirin must have done some good; the cold chills were gone and other than feeling a little woozy, she felt almost normal. She ought to call the kids back home, she thought guiltily.

Suddenly the front door squeaked long and low, opening with more stealth than her children ever exhibited.

She held her breath.

She scanned the cluttered bathroom for a weapon, but found only dirty clothes and towels, nothing that would serve in her defense. She lifted a dirty sock. If she could get it close enough to the prowler's nose...

"Cecil?" Jeff's voice floated down the hall.

She dropped the sock as if stung. What in blazes was he doing here? She swung open the bathroom door and saw his dark silhouette in the shadow of the foyer stairs.

"What do you think you're doing?" she spit out.

Jeff flipped on the light switch, and the yellow glare revealed his quizzical and bemused expression. A brown bag dangled from one hand; a soccer ball was tucked under his arm. His pearl gray shirt-sleeves were rolled back and his tie and suit jacket were missing. He fixed her with a slightly disapproving stare. "The door wasn't locked. Something tells me that Peter wouldn't approve."

"Yeah, well, you're right." Unreasonably irritated, she leaned against the doorjamb. "But, then, Peter doesn't approve of you, either."

"I noticed. I hope you don't mind my saying so, but the feelings are mutual." Jeff walked toward her.

She fumbled behind her and closed the bathroom door before he could see the mess inside. "Why are you here?" she asked as he stopped a few feet away.

"I got to the office and reached in the back seat for my briefcase and found this." He offered her the scuffed, dirty soccer ball. "According to my receptionist, it's an expensive one."

"Forty-nine dollars and ninety-five cents, before tax." Cecilia took it from him, trying to feel grateful. She tossed it at the wicker basket beside the front door, a good twenty feet away. It landed dead center. The basket rocked a bit, then settled.

"Swish," Jeff remarked grudgingly. "Nice aim."

"Lots of practice," she replied, rubbing her hands on the back side of her jeans. She tilted her head back. "I, uh, really appreciate all the trouble you've been to today."

"I thought . . . well, you seemed like you needed a little help." He aimed a quick glance into the den. "Where are the kids?"

"Next door with Carol."

"Oh, yeah. We met." He relaxed visibly and raised the brown bag. "I thought you might need something to eat."

"That's very generous of you, I'm sure." Cecilia took a shaky breath. "But as a matter of fact, I was going to call Carol and have her send the kids home. I feel much better now."

Jeff snorted. "Just what you need—Little Dillinger and the Keystone Kops."

Cecilia bristled. "I dare you to say that when I'm up to retaliating."

"Does he really balance your checkbook?" Jeff asked casually.

That damned checkbook again! "That's none of your business," she replied, raising her chin.

"Answer my question, Cecil. Does that kid really balance your checkbook?"

"As a matter of fact, yes." She raised her chin higher. Let him figure that one out. She stepped toward the door. "I know you're busy, and I do appreciate your concern, so—"

Jeff ignored her and strolled into the den. "The kitchen's this way, right?"

Cecilia spun around. "What are you doing?"

He set the grocery bag on the breakfast bar. "Chicken soup."

"Chicken soup?" Cecilia felt her mouth agape, and promptly shut it with a click of her teeth.

Jeff gave a tentative half smile. "I really need to be getting back to the office."

Cecilia brushed a tangle of curls away from her face. "Thank you. Very much."

"Anytime." His eyes quickly met hers in dismay. "I mean . . . for old times' sake."

Cecilia forced a brittle smile. He was certainly conscientious, the adult Mr. Jefferson Smith. He hadn't been able to ignore her plight, but he sure as heck couldn't wait to leave, either. "I'll bet you were a Boy Scout," she said sweetly. "You know the way out, but I'll walk you to the door. This time I want to make sure it's locked." She indicated the door with a jerk of her head, and gasped. The room tilted sideways; the floor vanished from beneath her. Her head roared, and the room whirled. She groped wildly, but felt herself falling. . . .

She hit the floor with a thud and found herself staring blearily at the immaculate creases in Jeff's pant legs—all five of them. "Oh, Lord." Desperately she tried to rise.

Jeff squatted beside her and pressed her shoulders firmly onto the carpet. "Just relax. Don't try to get up yet." He brushed damp curls from her forehead.

"I can't believe this," she moaned. Still light-headed, she closed her eyes and inhaled deeply.

"Just like old times, eh?"

She blinked up at him in consternation. "What?"

"You throwing yourself at my feet. Twice in the same day, no less," he teased. "Just like old times."

"I did not!" she protested, struggling to sit up. "I mean, back then I did, but today I certainly didn't!" She braced her hands against the floor. "I—I don't even want you here."

"You know, Cecil," he said sternly, his face inches from hers, "I'm not used to having the welcome mat jerked out from under my feet."

"I'll bet," Cecilia muttered, visualizing a string of svelte women eager to feed this man's arrogance. Why couldn't he have gone bald and potbellied?

"Okay, let me help you up."

Before she could protest, he closed his hands around her upper arms and lifted. She stood shakily and waited for the room to career wildly again. It didn't, but she sank gratefully into a barrel-backed bar stool.

"You're really sick, Cecilia."

She managed a smile. "I think the flu bug crawled into my inner ear."

"You need something in your stomach."

"Really, Jeff. Please go home, or back to work, or wherever it is you're supposed to be."

He began opening drawers in the kitchen, raking through their jumbled contents. "Where do you keep your can opener? I'll heat up the soup before I go."

"Yuk." She wrinkled her nose and massaged a temple wearily with the heel of her hand. "Did anyone ever bother to stick the pizza in the freezer?"

Jeff shot her a startled look. "Pizza?"

"Whenever I get sick I crave pizza."

"My granny would be appalled." He crossed to the refrigerator and opened the freezer compartment. "You're in luck. They're here. Hey, what do you know? I think I found your neighbor's scissors." He dropped two pizzas and a pair of orange-handled scissors on the counter. "Those scissors are freezing!" He rubbed his fingers vigorously on the seat of his trousers.

"Fancy that," Cecilia remarked dryly.

The phone rang and Jeff reached for it, but Cecilia lunged to her feet, motioning him away. "Let me answer it. It might be somebody," she gasped.

"Somebody?" He arched a brow and smiled, sliding the first pizza from its torn box.

"Hello.... Hi, Carol, how are the kids? ... Ralph, too? I didn't even notice he was gone. Much better, thanks. In fact, if you— What do you mean? Why shouldn't they look out the front window?... Red convertible? What red...oh, yeah." She shot a venomous glance at Jeff and dropped her voice. "It's a long story, Carol. Don't worry about it. It's leaving soon. By the way, we, er, I found your scissors in the freezer.... How would I know? They just were— Okay, you're an angel...I owe you one."

She replaced the receiver. Jeff was leaning against the counter, his arms folded. He was obviously taking everything in with far too great an interest. Then the slightest smile tugged at the corner of his mouth, and her stomach tugged in direct response. No, he wasn't smiling. The arrogant so-and-so was smirking at her. Instantly she felt fourteen years old again, and she didn't like it one bit.

"Since you're so interested, why didn't you get on the extension?" she muttered.

"I think I can fill in the blanks pretty well." Jeff doublechecked the setting on the oven, then glanced at the clock beside it. "Eleven more minutes. Think you can wait that long?" He smiled, a soft teasing kind of smile that stopped her dead in her tracks.

Those eyes, thick lashed and the color of root beer, crinkling at the corners... She'd forgotten how devastating his slow smile could be. She dragged herself back to reality. "All right, Florence Nightingale. I need a drink of water."

Jeff reached across the bar and pressed his hand to her temple.

She caught her breath, but tried not to show it.

"You must be feeling better. Your fever's down."

"Yeah, I know," she choked out, shrinking from his touch. "But I need some more aspirin." She clutched the edge of the counter.

"Would it do any good to ask where you keep the aspirin?" When she failed to respond he sighed. "I'm not surprised." He banged open cabinets and drawers until he found the elusive bottle. "Ahah! I should have known. In the drawer with the knives. I suppose if the aspirin doesn't do the trick, you go in for a little bloodletting?"

"Try murder," she gritted, and glared at the aspirin and water he offered.

"Bottoms up. Drink every drop. You need plenty of fluids."

Cecilia swallowed the medicine and thrust the glass at him. "Drink it yourself, Florence."

"I don't want your germs." His hand closed over hers, pinning her fingers against the glass. "Drink a little more."

The whole universe seemed to lurch, and she sank onto the bar stool again.

"All right," he muttered. "Enough is enough. You need to lie down."

She hadn't the strength to protest or struggle as he rounded the end of the bar and pulled her firmly off the stool. "Lean against me. It's all right." He eased her onto the sofa, then squatted beside her, studying her face intently.

She closed her eyes against his penetrating gaze. "I think I need that water now."

His chuckle vibrated through her. "I would be a real cad if I said 'I told you so.' "

"You're damn right."

He grinned. "I told you so."

"Just like old times." But her taunt had no sting. Rather, she felt a vague distress as he pulled away and stood up. She blamed her reaction on the cold—the cold that had crept back into her as soon as he wasn't there. She chafed her arms.

"Let me get you a blanket. Where do you keep them, in the refrigerator?"

"Cute, Jeff." She angled her head against a needlepoint pillow. Thinking of the jumble of sheets, blankets and sleeping bags that would tumble onto his head if he opened the linen closet, she said, "Get me the cover off Peter's bed. It's the top bunk in the bedroom on the left upstairs—I mean, right."

Shaking his head, he left, returning moments later with a faded blue afghan. She stiffened as he tucked it around her, then stifled a gasp when his knuckles brushed lightly against her chin.

"You know," he said, "it might help if you explained why having me here is upsetting you so much." He dropped down beside her, perching on the side of the sofa.

"You wouldn't understand," Cecilia said with a sigh.

"Try me."

"Look," she started, swallowed, then tried again. "Having you walk back into my life today makes me feel like I'm fourteen years old again. The first time was plenty, believe me. At this point in my life, I need a little maturity, and…and…" She struggled upright and looked him in the eye. "Dignity."

"Dignity?" Jeff eyed her doubtfully and guided her head firmly back to the pillow. "Keep your head down, kid. You're getting light-headed again."

"Just thinking about you is enough to make me break out in hives."

He arched his brows.

"Chasing you the way I did is the dumbest thing I've ever done in my life, and that's saying something!"

"You were kind of a pest," he agreed amiably, tracing a chain of stitches across the afghan with his index finger.

Cecilia felt her lower lip pulling into a pout and caught it with her teeth. "Frankly, Jeff, I was hoping you'd forget I ever existed. I've certainly done my best to forget you!"

His laughter should have made her angry; instead it warmed her right down to her toes. Eyes dancing, he replied, "Don't worry, I remember you. How could I forget? You made me a living legend. You should see some of the things the guys wrote under your picture in my yearbook. No, maybe that's not a good idea."

He laughed again as she buried her face in her hands and groaned. "Look, this is really cozy, but would you please let me up now? I'm getting a cramp in my leg."

"Whatever you say." He rose, then held out his hands.

Cecilia squirmed to a sitting position, then allowed him to pull her to her feet. Her head throbbed, and try as she might, she couldn't banish the spicy scent of his cologne from her senses. Breaking away from him, she rubbed her temples. "I don't feel so good."

"No, and you look worse."

She glared at him. "I think it's time you left."

"You're probably right. You'll eat something, then go straight back to bed when I'm gone, right?"

"I don't need a keeper or a nurse," she retorted. "As soon as I lock the door behind you, I'm going to take a bath."

"A bath? Are you crazy?"

"No, I'm not crazy! I happen to find hot baths therapeutic."

"In your condition? You're liable to pass out and go under. People have drowned in two inches of water, Cecilia."

She clenched her fists at her sides, and felt adrenaline giving her much needed strength. Be nice, Cecilia, she warned herself. Once every fifteen years, you can tolerate a little arrogance and undeserved authority. "Go back to work, Jeff, and leave me to drown in peace. I promise, I won't hold you responsible."

"Cecil, don't be ridiculous."

"Don't—" she gasped angrily, then fought down her rage "—don't call me ridiculous. Believe it or not, Jeff, I can manage without you."

He stared at her and she refused to look away. "If you feel that strongly about it . . . I'm sorry. I didn't mean to offend you. Go take your bath if you really think it will help you feel better. But I'm not leaving you here alone."

She moved to the door, then hesitated.

"Jeff?" She blushed. "If the phone rings, I'd rather you didn't answer it."

"That's fine with me. Of course, if Peter happens to look out the window and sees my car, he'll probably call to check up on us. And if nobody answers—well, I hate to think what he might do. He's liable to bring the Keystone Kops over to rescue you."

"Never mind," she said. "I suppose you're right." She glanced at the phone again, nibbling her lower lip. "Just take it off the hook. I'll be through in a jiffy."

"Whatever you say." He crossed the room and removed the receiver. "Is that better? Now be careful, and if you start to feel dizzy again, just call me."

"Over my dead body," she muttered.

Entering the bathroom, she was confronted by her reflection in the mirror. Shadowed eyes, hollowed cheeks, ashen skin. Even her Maverick sweatshirt had seen better days, and her jeans were downright ratty.

"Do you need help running the water?" he called.

"No!" She shut the door and locked it, then kicked aside the dirty clothes and made her way to the tub.

"Terrific," she groaned, jerking the sweatshirt over her head and flinging it to the floor.

Jeff leaned against the kitchen counter and was rather amazed to find himself smiling. He gave his head a wry shake, rubbing the bridge of his nose with a tanned finger. What had gotten into him? It had been a long time since he'd been this intrigued by a woman. And of all people, Cecilia Greene. Rather, Evans. Not his type at all.

What was it about that blazing mop of red hair, those big green eyes? He tried to shake her image out of his head, but he couldn't. Why couldn't he leave? Hell, he had groped at any excuse to stay.

The timer pinged and he crossed to the oven. He opened the door and stepped away from the blast of heat. The cheese bubbled, and the edges of the pepperoni curled. Where the devil would she keep pot holders? He was about to dig through the drawers again, when he spied one dangling from a magnetic hook on the refrigerator. He snatched it from its spot between a soccer schedule and a reminder to "DO IT NOW!"

As he maneuvered the pizza toward the front of the rack, he brushed his knuckles against the hot metal. Dropping the pot holder, he stifled a curse, then sucked gently at the burn.

"Well, sh—" he started, then clamped his mouth shut. He snatched the pot holder from where it landed on the bottom of the oven and slung it onto the counter, then used a pancake turner to ease the pizza onto a plate.

As he placed the plate on the counter, Jeff's attention was diverted to the pot holder. It had landed plain-side down, so that now he could see the shape of a small hand on it, and the inscription, "PETER, 5 years old." The side he hadn't noticed before. He lifted a corner and stared at the brown burn permanently branding Peter's palm print.

"You weren't supposed to use that one."

Jeff whirled toward the source of the small, childish voice. "Which—which one are you?"

The redheaded imp cocked his head. "Brad."

Jeff eyed the eight-year-old warily. "I thought you were next door."

"Peter made me come home to brush my teeth. He thinks just because he's oldest, he's the boss." Brad hooked the pot holder in place, flipping the singed side toward the refrigerator. "Don't worry, Mom'll never notice."

Jeff rubbed his hands on the rough wale of his trousers. "Would you, er, would you like some pizza?" Not waiting for a response, he grabbed a knife out of the aspirin drawer and sawed the pizza into precise portions.

Brad propped his elbows on the counter to watch. "Uhh-uhh...if I don't get back pretty quick, Peter'll come lookin' for me."

"By all means," Jeff mumbled around a bite of pizza. "Don't let me keep you."

"He doesn't like you," Brad offered straight-faced, an impish twinkle in his eyes. Eyes just like his mother's.

Jeff bit off another hunk of pizza to avoid answering.

"Well, I guess I'll go get my toothbrush."

Jeff watched him lope across the room, then blurted out, "You can't."

The boy spun around, facing Jeff quizzically.

"Your mom's taking a bath," Jeff explained awkwardly.

"Oh?" Brad seemed to consider that for a moment, then brightened and shrugged. "That means I have time for pizza."

The threat Cecilia's eldest son, or worse, the arrival of a horde of screaming children, gave Jeff indigestion. "Look, buddy, let me see your teeth."

Brad bared his incisors for inspection.

"Who told you these teeth were dirty? They look fine to me."

"That's what I said," Brad complained. "But Peter said—"

"Look, just go on back over there, take this pizza with you, and I'll ask your mom if she wants you to brush your teeth. If she does, she'll call you back home."

"Hey, that's great!" Brad grabbed the plate and headed for the back door. Hands full, he waited for Jeff to let him out. "Peter's not gonna like you bein' here."

Jeff snorted. "So don't tell him."

A grin widened across his freckled face. "Okay." He hesitated at the door and squinted at Jeff. "You know that pot holder? Mom'll never notice, but Peter will."

Cecilia paused as she entered the den. Jeff sat on the couch, holding a slice of pizza and a can of beer. "I hope you don't mind. I made myself at home."

"Is there any pizza left, or have you scarfed it all down?"

Jeff sprang to his feet. "I'm supposed to be taking care of you. Just sit down. I'll fix you some."

Cecilia dropped into the nearest chair.

"Nope." Jeff grabbed her arm and pulled her up. "That's not good enough. Come sit on the sofa. You need to relax."

Cecilia allowed him to guide her, and not until she dropped onto the soft leather couch did she realize how much she needed to lie down. Jeff shook out the afghan, then tossed it over her reclining body, letting it settle with a soft whoosh. "Isn't that better?"

"Hmmph." She refused to give him the satisfaction.

"Want a beer?" Smiling at her grimace, he answered his own question. "I didn't think so." He struggled with the pizza, forcing the knife through its asphalt-shingle crust. "You don't approve of beer?"

Her eyes slid away from his. "There just hasn't been any beer around here lately. Your question startled me, that's all." She rubbed her nose self-consciously and reached for a slice of pizza. "This is cold."

"Cold pizza's good for the soul." Jeff eased to the floor beside her and resumed eating.

Cecilia watched him from the corner of her eye. Stretched out on the floor, he looked almost the same as the first time she'd seen him . . . long legs, wide shoulders and that same arrogant cleft in his chin. She leaned against the soft cushion and sighed. If there was one thing she didn't need, it was another male around the house.

Especially not if that male was Jefferson Smith.

He cleared his throat awkwardly. "I realize that this has been an exceptionally bad day for you."

"It comes with the territory. If you walked into this house a hundred times, ninety-nine of them would be as crazy as today." A stubborn defiance was reflected in the eyes she raised to him. "They're good kids. A little unorthodox, maybe, but then..." She shrugged. "Combine heredity with environment, and what could you expect?"

"Every time I think how much you've changed, I realize how much you haven't." His lips twisting in a wry smile, Jeff leaned back on his palms and cocked his head curiously. "What do you do to hold things together?"

"I sing."

Jeff narrowed his eyes suspiciously. "You . . . sing?"

"That's what I said."

"Sing what?"

"Commercial jingles for radio. I've done some voice-overs for a couple of television commercials, mainly local stuff. And weekends I usually sing with a dance band."

Jeff laughed. "You're not kidding, are you?"

"No, I'm not kidding." Her feathers a bit ruffled, Cecilia squirmed to a sitting position and curled her feet beneath her, holding the old afghan snug around her shoulders.

"Anything I'd recognize?"

This was the part Cecilia always hated. Her list of credits included radio jingles that were heard all over the country, but most of her local work was low-budget commercials, not the kind of resumé to impress people who knew nothing about the business. "Probably not."

Jeff studied her closely. "Is that a particularly lucrative line of work?"

"I manage quite well as a matter of fact."

"So well that you're overdrawn."

"Not often, only occasionally." She could explain about the other account, but chose to let him think the worst. "It's really none of your business, is it? But I have a check in my purse I've been carrying around since last Thursday, and I still haven't made it by the bank."

"You're kidding me, aren't you?" he asked, his expression incredulous.

"Will you stop gawking at me? No, I'm not kidding."

Jeff gulped. "No wonder little Dillinger yells at you."

"I should have known you'd take his side," she grumbled.

"I'll tell you what. Let me take a look at that checkbook. The least I can do is straighten it out for you."

"You aren't touching my checkbook, Jeff Smith," she snapped.

"Cecilia, don't be offended. I'm a CPA. I have my own firm. It's my business to straighten out people's financial messes. Strictly business."

"I'm not impressed, and you're not touching my checkbook," Cecilia growled. "Anyway, Peter balanced it this afternoon."

He rolled his eyes and hoisted himself up from the floor. "This I've gotta see."

"Absolutely not," she responded sharply. "Peter's perfectly capable of balancing my checkbook. As a matter of fact, he could probably handle the accounts payable of Chase Manhattan Bank."

"That's difficult to believe, Cecilia."

"So, don't believe it. I don't have to prove it, because it's none of your business," she repeated.

"No wonder the kid's such a pain. He's probably thoroughly convinced that no one on earth's his equal."

"Sound familiar?" Cecilia taunted, taking pleasure in the ruddy stain that crept up Jeff's neck. "A certain senior I knew once had the same tendencies—in spades."

He laughed then, a velvet sound that tingled from her scalp to her toes. Eyes glowing, he reached for her hand and moved to her side again. "One thing I have to say for you, kid. There never was a dull moment when you were around. And you haven't changed a bit."

"We are a rather diverting bunch," Cecilia agreed, slumping back onto the cushions and dropping his hand. Now it made sense. He was bored and lonely, probably between playmates, and had decided to check out ol' Cecil for grins—kind of like a trip to the zoo.

She studied him with more calm than she felt. "Jeff, I don't know how to say this, but I can't avoid it." She drew in a deep breath and then finally voiced the fear that had haunted her all day. "This has been a very strange day for me. Oh, I'm not talking about checkbooks or the kids, or even being sick. I'm talking about you." Flustered, she caught her breath. She raised her burning green eyes to his surprised brown ones feeling rather foolish.

"Cecilia Evans, are you giving me the brush-off?" His features transformed slowly from confusion to surprise. "You're afraid of me."

"Why should I be afraid?" she asked, forcing out the words, her voice husky. "I just don't have time for..."

"For what?" There was curiosity in his eyes, curiosity and expectancy. That elusive question hung between them, and he seemed as ill at ease as she felt.

He raised his face to hers, and she instinctively touched her hands to the sides of his head. She felt herself trembling as if on the edge of a precipice, fearing the plunge even as she longed for the push that would send her over the edge.

"Don't do this to me." She squeezed her eyes shut, dropping her hands to her sides and digging them into the rough afghan to erase the memory of his hair from her fingertips. "Do I have to hit you over the head with a brickbat? You don't fit in here! I don't want you here!"

Jeff pulled away, stunned. She watched the confusion on his face, watched it harden, watched him retreat behind a composed expression. Too composed. And at that moment, she felt a stabbing pain of remembrance because she saw such a remarkable resemblance to the young Jefferson Smith.

"Maybe you're right," he said. Then, with a smile that creased sharp edges around his mouth yet never reached his eyes, he said, "I think I'd better be going. But it's the craziest thing. When you think back on that year you say it was humiliating. When I remember that year I remember wanting to tie you up and dump you in the Trinity River."

He seemed a little embarrassed, a little confused. "But now... well, it doesn't seem so bad now. It's the damnedest thing, but that year seems kind of special."

He moved about the room, and a chill settled over her. His movements were quick and precise as he cleaned up the debris from their dinner, systematically erasing every indication that he had been in the house, even putting the empty beer cans in his own grocery bag to take home with his soup.

Her blunt nails dug into her palms as she fought back the conciliatory words that sprang to her lips. She knew his leaving was for the best. After all, he was only doing what she wanted him to.

Why didn't she feel relieved?

Jeff stood over her with his brown bag clutched in one hand. She looked up at his towering height with deeper regret than she dared admit, even to herself.

"Are you feeling all right?" he asked quietly. "I could call your friend."

"No." She brushed a strand of hair away from her face. "I'll be fine."

He grasped her hand firmly and pulled her to her feet. "Walk me to the door," he ordered. "This time I want the dead bolt locked."

As he moved away from her, Cecilia fought the impulse to reach out and stop him. What was wrong with her? She didn't want him there, yet she did. It was because she was sick, she told herself. That's all. Weak and sick and vulnerable.

At the front door she refused to raise her eyes to his. "Thanks for everything," she whispered numbly.

"For old times," he answered, then left. She locked the dead bolt and leaned her forehead against the cool surface of the door, listening to his steps fade away. Suddenly the sound of his retreat seemed strangely foreboding. She pushed away from the door and hurried back through the house, flipping off lights as she went. She fell into bed with a sigh of relief...an empty sigh.

She didn't need a man. She certainly didn't need Jeff. She only needed a good night's sleep to banish the curious and hollow ache from her heart.

Three

An army was pounding down the door with a battering ram, not to mention dingdonging the damned doorbell off the wall. Cecilia tumbled out of bed and stumbled down the hallway, her head feeling somewhat to the east of the rest of her body. Somebody had better be ready for a few choice words. She swung the door open, winced at the bright sunshine, and was confronted by the kids and Ralph.

Carol stood behind them, gesturing helplessly. "I tried to stop them, Cecilia, I really did. But I couldn't keep them away." She cast an uneasy glance over her shoulder. "I have to admit, I'm surprised. I'm not criticizing, mind you, but I'm very surprised."

Peter pushed sullenly past Cecilia and stalked into the house, Brad and Anne-Elizabeth following hot on his heels.

"What are you talking about, Carol?" Cecilia leaned back against the doorjamb and cradled her head in her hands.

"Well, you certainly are cool about it, I'll hand you that." Carol peered cautiously into the house.

"Cool about what? I don't know what you're talking about," Cecilia repeated.

"Well, honey, I managed to keep the kids in the back of the house last night, but really! How was I to know he'd still be here this morning? When the kids saw his car..."

Cecilia jerked her head up. "What do you mean? Jeff left before ten last night." Without waiting, she pushed past her friend and flew down the front steps. Parked innocently behind the red Suburban was Jeff's red convertible. Cecilia threw her hands to her forehead and shrieked, "What is it doing here?"

Carol came quickly to her side. "It's okay, Cecilia. Don't have a conniption. I'm sure there's a perfectly logical explanation for this." She didn't sound convinced, though. "You mean he's really not in the house?"

Cecilia puffed up with indignation. "Carol, do you mean to tell me that you honestly thought... Carol! How could you?" she wailed. "And the kids, what are they doing? Checking the beds?"

"Calm down, honey," Carol begged. "I should have known better." She glanced at the neighbor's house across the street just in time to see a curtain fall back in place. "Come back in the house. You're attracting attention."

"I'm attracting attention? I'm not the one who left this—this—dune buggy parked in front of my house all night!"

"That happens to be a very expensive sports car, and standing here screaming about it is not going to make it disappear," Carol said firmly. "Now let's go calmly into the house..."

"Calmly? Calmly, you say? I'm supposed to go calmly into the house—" her voice was deceptively low "—while this very expensive sports car sits in my driveway, announcing to all the neighbors that I had a man spend the night with me last night?" By the time she'd finished her voice had reached a shrill peak, and she marched over to the car and kicked the rear tire for good measure.

Carol followed after her. "But Cecilia, you said he didn't spend the night here last night."

"Of course he didn't!" Cecilia whirled on her friend. "Don't you believe me?"

"You know I believe you."

"Okay. Wonderful. So let's analyze this situation very carefully." She began to tick her conclusions off on her fingers. "One, you know I slept alone last night. Two, I know I slept alone last night. Three, the kids know it, because by now they have turned the house upside down looking for—for—" She rushed on, unable to complete the thought. "But—and this is a major but—" she thrust both hands into the air "—everyone else in the world thinks I had a man in my bed!"

"Mom," Brad called from the front porch, "did you know you left the phone off the hook? No wonder we couldn't get you this morning."

Cecilia thought back to the night before. "The idiot didn't even hang up the phone after I got out of the bath," she spat out, oblivious to Carol's startled look. "Thank you, Brad. Did you hang it up?"

"Yeah, but it rang right off. Some man wants to talk to you." He watched with interest as the thundercloud settled over his mother's face.

"Some man, huh? Did he happen to say who he is?"

"Not to me, but Anne-Elizabeth's talking to him now." Brad followed her into the house. Carol didn't even hesitate to join them, unabashedly curious.

Entering the den, Cecilia saw Anne-Elizabeth sitting on the breakfast bar, chattering into the telephone. "She's in the fwont yard kickin' a car," she confided to the unknown party. "She's scweamin', too."

"Anne-Elizabeth, give me that phone," Cecilia threatened.

The little girl stared at her stubbornly, but released the phone to her mother's trembling hand. "Mommy's mad, and I didn't do it," Anne-Elizabeth said to no one in particular as she scrambled down from the bar and took refuge behind Ralph.

"Hello." Her fist tightened when she heard Jeff's voice.

"Cecil, I can explain everything." He sounded worried, very worried.

"Explain everything, Jeff?" Her tone of voice dripped arsenic-laced honey. "Why, whatever do you mean?"

"Now, Cecil. I don't know why you're so upset. After all, it's my car that won't start."

"If there weren't children in the room, I would be very glad to tell you why I am so upset, Mr. Smith." She spoke through clenched teeth. "But I refuse to subject their innocent ears to the kinds of things I would like to say under these circumstances."

"I told ya he was a jerk," Peter snorted. "Come on, Brad, let's get out of here so she can blast him." Carol dragged Ralph and a very unwilling Anne-Elizabeth behind her, and within seconds the room had cleared.

Cecilia interrupted Jeff in mid-sentence. "I will give you one hour to get that car out of my driveway. If it's not gone by then, I'm going to call a tow truck. Is that clear?"

"Wait just a minute, Cecil. You didn't really kick my car, did you? Do you have any idea how much that car is worth? I spent hours rebuilding that car. It's a classic! And if you so much as scratch it, you'll be sorry."

"Them move it!"

"What's the problem? We're talking about a car that won't start. I don't believe that's a criminal offense in the continental United States, Hawaii, Alaska, or the territories!"

"Use your brains—you're supposed to be so smart! Your car was parked in front of my house all night. Do you realize what that looks like? And you didn't even have the common decency to warn me."

"Good grief, Cecil. I stayed out there a half hour trying to get the thing to start, and by then you'd long turned out the lights. I figured you'd rather sleep than be bothered."

"Well, Jeff, you thought wrong. I realize that being a swinging bachelor—a man of the world, shall we say?—you wouldn't be accustomed to thinking about things like that. Perhaps the women you usually associate with don't have reputations to protect, but in my case I can assure you—"

"Okay, okay, I get the point," he broke in roughly. "Look, I'll have the car moved before dark. In case you're interested, it wasn't my idea of a fun evening to walk five blocks to a convenience store and call a friend to pick me up."

"My heart bleeds for you." She tossed her head impatiently, and the room suddenly spun. "What...what are you going to do about your car? You're blocking me in."

"I'll get that car moved if I have to carry it. But listen to me carefully." She heard his ragged breath, and realized that the menace in his voice was very real. "You don't go near my car with a tow truck. Is that clear?"

"Perfectly," she snapped.

"And keep those kids of yours away from it, too."

"Don't worry," Cecilia replied coolly. "They have Hot Wheels with more class than that junk heap."

"Junk? Have you no taste?"

"Unfortunately, no. I fell for you, didn't I?"

"Don't remind me. That was the beginning of my troubles."

"All you need to do is move your little car, and then your troubles will be over, at least as far as I'm concerned," Cecilia announced, then slammed the phone down.

The telephone rang.

"Hello," she answered, striving to keep her voice cool.

"Cecilia Evans, you have more hang-ups than a nutty fourteen-year-old I used to know, and that's saying plenty!"

The phone clicked in her ear.

Jeff shoved himself away from the pay telephone, the wiry muscles in his forearms knotting with tension. Who the hell did she think she was, giving him orders? What he really ought to do was go on over there immediately.

He glanced at his watch, conscious of the overdue twenty-six laps waiting for him. Twenty-six laps he would have run Thursday evening, if he hadn't worked late. Twenty-six laps he would have run last night if he hadn't gone to Cecil's. His fists bunched in exasperation.

He took the stairs to the jogging track two at a time, then plunged into the Saturday morning "traffic" with a score of other masochists who resorted to running to keep their middles slim and their arteries clear.

Damn, she was the most troublesome female he'd ever encountered in his entire life, he thought, methodically placing one foot in front of the other, his elbows pumping rhythmically with each step. Some things never changed. At fourteen Cecil had been incorrigible, and now, as if one Cecilia Evans in the world wasn't bad enough, matters were even worse. Not only was she still trouble with a capital *T*, she had cloned three incorrigible kids.

He remembered his car, his pride and joy, at the mercy of Cecil's clan, and stumbled.

He stifled the urge to toss off the entire day and go rescue his car immediately. One lap down, twenty-five to go.

Besides, what could they really do to his car?

Two laps later, he'd thought of a half-dozen things they could do to the exterior alone. That hard, red finish would be a prime target for anything from graffiti to Tic-Tac-Toe. They could slash the tires, the rag top...

He was being ridiculous. Of course they wouldn't do any of those things. They might be brats, but they weren't delinquents.

Five laps. He concentrated on the people in the weight rooms flanking the track, his eyes trained on the males as he ran one side and the females as he completed the circle. Overhead, speakers amplified a bland male voice as it encouraged those on the machines, "Ready, begin." Sixty seconds and three-quarters of a lap later, "You're halfway through." And then, "Finished. Move to the next machine." And like sweating automatons, the club's patrons, male and female alike, abandoned one gleaming instrument of torture and moved on to the next. A completed circuit was supposed to work every muscle in the body.

Jeff swiped the sweat out of his eyes. Not for him such lunacy. Of course, he was nobody to talk. He'd paid through the nose for a health club that boasted saunas, a lap pool, three weight rooms and an aerobic area—all of which he ignored to run two miles, three times a week, like a mindless rat on a treadmill. White Rock Lake would be closer, cheaper, more scenic. He grabbed his side and forced the air into his lungs. In, out. In, out. One foot in front of the other.

But who gave a damn about scenic when it was raining or, worse, sleeting? Who needed fresh air? He didn't. Besides, he thought, rounding the north end of the track for the twelfth time. Here he knew exactly where two miles ended. Not one step too many, not one step too few. From the first day he'd forced himself to finish the entire run, and again on the second, when his aching muscles had made it even worse. Two years, and he hadn't missed a run or short-changed a lap.

Thirteen down, thirteen to go.

Two years, and his lung capacity had increased, his waist had slimmed and his color had improved.

Six hundred twenty-four miles later, he still wasn't sure it was worth it.

The slender woman in front of him wore red shorts. He didn't usually notice things like that by this point in his run, but it was the exact shade of red as his car. His baby. His pride and joy.

He forced his fists to relax. Only ten more laps. He tried to unclench his jaw. But instead of red nylon, he was seeing the immaculate red finish of his car. Scratched by a bicycle, or perhaps a dog's claws. His windshield shattered by a stray baseball.

A quarter way through the fourteenth lap, he did an abrupt U-turn and headed for the stairs, swerving around the scowling runners now headed straight toward him.

Four minutes later, damp from his shower, he tugged on his jeans. As he zipped up, he caught a glimpse of himself in the mirror. His stomach was definitely flatter, even without sit-ups. But why was he noticing such a thing at this late date?

He tugged a knit shirt over his head and slipped on a poplin jacket, shoving his sweaty running gear into his duffel bag, ready to make a mad dash for Cecil's and his car.

Another glance in the mirror revealed his hair, still wet, pressed against his head. He snatched a towel out of his bag and rubbed it halfway dry. After all, he couldn't afford to catch some damned virus. He had taxes to figure, forms to fill. Again he grabbed his bag and headed for the door.

He stopped to comb his hair, and tried to convince himself it was the general public he was trying to impress.

Certainly not Cecilia Evans.

Never in a million years.

* * *

Humming along with the radio, Cecilia grabbed a wicker basket of magazines from the floor beside the easy chair and unceremoniously dumped them onto the coffee table. Methodically she gathered the baseball cards, Hot Wheels and army men into the basket, stifling a curse when her bare foot landed on a plastic bayonet.

The basket was almost full but the carpet still littered, when she noticed Peter in the doorway. "You really told that jerk off, didn't you?"

"I'd rather not discuss it," she muttered, spying Ron Darling's grinning image under the sofa. She dropped to her knees to retrieve the card.

"I thought you were sick."

"I am." She thrust the basket into his hands. "Dump this mess in Brad's toy box, and come back for more." Then, after a second thought, she lifted Ron from the top of the pile. "He deserves better," she explained, slipping the picture of the sexy pitcher's grinning face into her back pocket.

When Peter returned, she tossed two more handfuls of boyish collectibles into the basket. "You finish the floor while I get the vacuum."

"If you're sick, why don't you go to bed?" Peter demanded.

"Mothers don't go to bed. They just keep on truckin'."

"Mom!"

Something in the tone of his voice stopped her in midstride. She pivoted, resting one hand on the door frame.

"Why are you wearing makeup?"

She flushed. "I just felt like it."

Peter snorted his disbelief, but began snatching the toys from the floor. Cecilia retrieved the vacuum cleaner from the hall closet.

Peter met her in the doorway. The floor was clean. Even the magazines were back in their basket. "Thanks," she said, planting a kiss on his forehead.

"Do you want me to vacuum?"

"No, no . . . you run on and play." She stooped to plug in the Hoover.

"I'm going to ride my bike, unless you want me to stay and keep the kids out of your hair."

She rose slowly and turned, digging her fingers into the small of her back. But her mind wasn't on her backache. Instead she stared at her eldest son in surprise. *The kids?* Didn't he consider himself one of them? Sadly she noticed the solemn expression in his gray eyes. Of all of them, the divorce had seemed to affect him the least, and had, of course, affected him the most.

"No, Peter," she answered slowly. "I'll be all right. You go off and play with your friends. I'll keep Brad and Anne-Elizabeth here with me. Don't you have soccer practice this afternoon?"

Peter shrugged. "Coach called and said to be there at one, but with that jerks's car blocking ours, I figured I'd have to miss."

"Don't worry, you'll be there. Now go on and play, okay?"

His shoulders relaxed. "Okay."

"Peter." She chucked him under the chin. "You're a good kid. A pain in the neck sometimes, but a good kid."

"Oh, yeah? I'll bet you say that to all the guys." He couldn't hide his grin as he dashed through the front door and down the steps.

She steeled herself for the coming encounter with Jefferson Smith. Just let him collect his car and check out of her life. That was all she asked, just a simple ending to a very complicated thirty-six hours.

An hour later, the doorbell rang. She counted to ten, walked calmly down the hall and fluffed the curls around her face before opening the door.

"Hello." She smiled, her tone cool and polite, just as she'd practiced. "Would you like to come in?"

Jeff shifted his toolbox impatiently from one hand to the other. "No, thanks. If it's all the same to you, I'll see what I can do to my alternator and get my car out of your way." His voice matched hers.

He bounced down the steps, and she watched the way his hips moved as he crossed the yard; watched the easy way his shoulders strained as he dropped his large toolbox in the

grass, then ran a hand lovingly down the length of the car.
She caught herself watching and slammed the door.

For the next hour Cecilia paced through the house,
squinting through various front windows to check on Jeff's
progress. For ten minutes, she sat on the edge of Peter's
immaculate desk, propping her elbow on the computer she'd
never tried to figure out, and gazed down on the top of
Jeff's glossy brown head. She wasn't the only one drawn to
watch his activities. Jeff was surrounded by curious neighborhood boys who had stopped by to examine his classic '57
Thunderbird throughout the day.

She noticed the studious effort it took for him to avoid
talking to his audience. Instead he trained all his attention
on his car. As the arrangement of screws, tools and parts
grew in a very carefully laid-out sweep beside the car, Cecilia fretted that he would never be able to reassemble the
jigsaw puzzle.

Enough of this nonsense, Cecilia, she ordered herself. She
flipped on the vacuum cleaner and zigzagged it over the
carpet.

She was shuffling through the jungle of military and
sports paraphernalia that served as furnishings for Brad's
bedroom, fighting the urge to peek through the camouflage
curtains at Jeff's wide shoulders straining beneath his damp
T-shirt, when the phone rang.

It took four rings before she could dash across the littered floor, down the stairs and to the hall phone. Cradling
the receiver between her neck and jaw, she answered.

"Hey, Toots, that you?"

She would have sighed if she'd had any breath left. "Hi,
Stan."

"You didn't forget about tonight, did you?"

"How could I forget seventy-five bucks?"

"Why couldn't I have found a songbird who sang for
love?"

"Why couldn't I have found a band that paid decent
wages?" she countered, chuckling in spite of herself. "Okay,
Stan. I'll be there, but I may be running a little late."

"Sure thing, toots. We'll be instrumental background for
the first set, anyway. See ya then."

She winced as she hung up the phone. Her back ached, her neck felt as though it had been carrying a double yoke for at least four furlongs, and spending another Saturday night providing wallpaper music for a well-fed assembly of celebrating executives and their wives held no appeal.

When the doorbell chimed, she was relieved to be spared her own self-pity, even if it was only to confront Jefferson Smith one more time. One last time, she reminded herself firmly, and tried to feel good about it.

She opened the door and, sure enough, Jeff was waiting for her, his hair ruffled, a black smudge on a high cheekbone and a general expression of relief on his even features. "I just wanted you to know I'm finished." His hands were smeared with grease halfway up his forearms. "I hate to bother you again, but . . ."

"You need to wash up." Cecilia hesitated two beats longer than seemed polite. She swung the door open wide and stepped out of his way. "The bathroom's at the end of the hall," she instructed, then flushed. "You remember."

He flashed a smile, his dimples bracketing his mouth with rakish charm. "I remember." Holding his hands aloft like a surgeon awaiting gloves, he lifted his eyebrows. "I think you'd better go with me, unless you want grease all over everything."

"No, I certainly don't want grease all over everything," she agreed, thinking of the time she'd already spent scrubbing the bathroom that very morning.

She flipped on the bathroom light, reached across him and turned on the faucet. "You may as well stand there a minute." She sighed. "These cranky pipes give hot water when they're good and ready."

She stood awkwardly as Jeff's gaze scanned the spacious L-shaped bathroom, skimming the ancient tile, the original pedestal sink, a chaise lounge beneath the narrow stained glass window.

His eyes stopped at the tub around the corner. Gleaming red, the antique-style tub stood on gnarled brass claw feet and sprouted brass handles and faucets.

"Nice touch," he said, grinning.

Cecilia leaned against the wall, wondering why she should feel so pleased at his approval. "You really like it? Robert almost killed me for buying it. I blew the whole bathroom budget on that one fixture." She pointed at the running faucet. "Hence the faulty plumbing."

"I can picture it in the winter, hot and steamy, maybe a little bubble bath, perfect for soaking."

She shrugged. "Robert would have preferred a whirl-pool. Roomier, and massage included."

"Oh, I don't know." He propped his hip against the sink, his brown eyes twinkling. "I can think of more intriguing ways to stir up the water than jet sprays."

"I'll bet." Turning her back to him, she grabbed a bar of heavy-duty soap and an old washcloth from the cabinet above the toilet. A quick adjustment and the water was hot enough to melt grease without scalding his skin, and she moved halfway out the door. "If you need anything else just holler." She hid her smirk from him. "And don't forget to clean up after yourself."

When Jeff finally emerged, his hair was damp around his freshly scrubbed face, his T-shirt had several wet splotches on it and his hands still bore a fine greasy residue under the nails. It seemed as if he were peeling off years every time she saw him, and it was all she could do not to send him back to the bathroom to wash off the smudge he'd missed near his left ear. His gaze lowered to her car keys. "Sorry I had you blocked all day. The kids said you had someplace to go."

At that moment Peter came whizzing into the driveway on his ten-speed. He managed to get it onto the porch, lock it to the brick post and push past his mother's visitor without looking once in Jeff's direction. "Come on, Mom, we're going to be late." He retrieved a soccer ball from under an azalea bush and herded his siblings toward the Suburban with ungentle pushes.

Cecilia locked the door and made as if to follow, but Jeff stopped her with a hand upon her shoulder. He splayed two fingers and touched the shadows beneath her eyes. "You ought to be in bed."

Her breath lodged in her throat. She stepped back, breaking the contact, but still he hovered above her.

"Have you gotten any rest at all today?"

"Yes, of course." And she wasn't really lying, not exactly. She had lain on the floor for a full side of a Streisand album, calling it research, when actually it had been a desperate attempt to shore up her energies before plunging back into the housework. But that was the way her life was these days. Every moment had to be justified. Every activity had to have a purpose, or else she was eaten alive by the guilt of knowing how much remained to be done.

She stared up into his sable-fringed, gold-flecked eyes. He was so much more accessible now that he was clothed in faded jeans and a T-shirt rather than custom-tailored silk. The accountant may not have totally transformed into a mechanic, but the blend was strangely comfortable. It was difficult to remember why she had been so angry with him; was it only this morning?

The horn honked. "I've got to go," she muttered, and he allowed her to pass in front of him. All the way to the car she was conscious of his easy strides following her. She slid into the driver's seat of the Suburban, and Jeff was there to shut the door.

"Take care," he said, then walked back toward his own car.

"Everybody buckled in?" Cecilia checked the kids in the back seat, and ended up watching Jeff swing his lean body into the low sports car. Not shabby, she thought with a twinge of regret. Not shabby at all. She sighed and snapped her own belt closed, then pumped the pedal and turned the key in the ignition.

Nothing happened.

She tried again, and pumped harder on the accelerator. Still nothing. "Don't tell me..." She rubbed the back of her neck. One more time...and one more nothing. Not a grind, not a groan, certainly not a purr like the one coming from Jeff's jewel of a car.

And then he was beside her again, bending over to better observe her newest catastrophe. "Is something wrong?"

"I don't know," she answered in clipped tones.

"Maybe you'd better let me have a look at it."

"No, no. You have things to do. I'll take care of it." He really must think she was incompetent, or certainly in dire need of a keeper. She certainly didn't want to owe him anything else.

Jeff looked intently at the dashboard. "Open the door," he commanded.

Cecilia opened it without enthusiasm and watched in dismay as he reached in and punched the headlight control; it clicked off.

"You must have left them on after you drove home in the rain yesterday."

Cecilia looked from his amused face to Peter's crushed expression. Following her gaze, Jeff sighed. "Where's he supposed to be?"

"At soccer practice," Brad piped up from the back seat. "And he's gonna be late."

Jeff expelled a deep breath. "Okay, kiddo, hop in my car. I'll take you." Peter started to argue, but Jeff had already headed back to his car.

"Go ahead, Peter. It's okay," Cecilia urged, attempting to conceal her frustration.

"I don't want to." His young jaw was set with a determination reminiscent of her own.

"Look, Peter, you're already late, so don't argue with me. You can catch a ride home with the coach after practice, but you have to get there first. So, vamoose!"

He hesitated, then loped self-consciously toward Jeff's car. Brad leaped from the Suburban and tossed him the soccer ball. "You almost forgot it, dummy!"

"Mom!" Peter protested.

"Don't call your brother a dummy, dummy." She ruffled Brad's carrot top and waved as the sports car pulled out of the driveway.

"Lucky dog," Brad muttered as they drove away.

"You know what your problem is, Cecilia?" Carol sat on the corner of Cecilia's unmade bed. "You have a mental block."

Cecilia paused, makeup brush poised over the ridge of a cheekbone, and swiveled away from the vanity. "A mental block regarding what?"

"That gorgeous man, honey, that gorgeous man," Carol drawled. "Why are you being so stubborn? If I were in your shoes, I'd be ecstatic!"

"If I never hear from him again, it'll suit me perfectly," Cecilia responded grimly, turning back to the mirror and brushing a rose blush onto her pale skin. "If you had any idea the memories he brings back, you'd understand. I was a total idiot. And I don't like having a constant reminder of my past humiliations hanging around."

"There!" Carol exclaimed. "That's exactly what I'm talking about! You can't see the guy for what he is because you're still too busy remembering what he was. If that hunk had been a stranger when he bailed you out of trouble with the police, you wouldn't be having these misgivings."

"In the first place, I wasn't in trouble. In the second place, he didn't bail me out. And in the third..." Cecilia leaned closer to the mirror and deftly applied a false eyelash to her right eye, then to her left. "If he had been a stranger, he never would have followed me in the first place, would he?" She blinked vampishly, considering the overall effect. A far sight different from the harried image that had confronted her only minutes before. "Hand me my dress, will you?"

Carol tossed the slithery red outfit to her. She ducked into it, and as it slid down her body, she couldn't help wondering what if she'd been dressed like this when she'd seen Jeff? She could picture herself as he'd seen her, tattered jeans and sweatshirt. But in red silk, with her topknot of auburn curls brushing against his shoulder... She wouldn't have encouraged him, of course. But at least she would have projected her hard-won independence, her self-confidence. Instead she had come across like a helpless idiot.

"You're thinking about him, Cecilia. I can tell." Carol didn't even try to disguise her smirk. "If you'd just be sensible."

"But you aren't talking sense. I know you mean well, but—" Ralph went into a frenzy of barking by the front door, and Cecilia's heart skipped a beat. "Peter must be back."

"Maybe 'tall, dark and gorgeous' brought him home."

That thought had already flitted through her mind. Which had nothing to do with the fact that she was hurrying toward the front door, just in case.

But Peter entered, alone and disgruntled. "What a jerk!"

"Your coach?" Cecilia queried.

"Your old friend," Peter sneered.

Cecila flinched. "What did he do?"

Peter shot her a dirty look, his pale brows lowered. "He dumped me and left, which is exactly what I wanted. But he's still a jerk." He noted her dress with a resigned expression. "You singin' tonight?"

"I'm afraid so."

"Well, you don't have to worry about that jerk coming around here any more."

"Peter Evans, what have you done?" she demanded.

He spread his hands wide, the picture of innocence. "Nothing. Not a thing."

Four

—

Jeff leaned into his town-house door and shoved gently; it gave with little pressure and opened soundlessly. But despite his caution, his arrival didn't go unnoticed.

"Give 'em hell," a grating voice drawled.

"Can it, Toulouse." He dropped his briefcase atop the walnut breakfront with a half-hearted sigh and hung his trench coat in the coat closet amidst a cacophony of screeches and squawks. He grabbed a sharp, carbon steel knife from the rack on the kitchen wall and a mango from the fruit bowl on the counter and proceeded into the living room.

"Give 'em hell, Harry!" a hoarse voice squawked.

"I'll give you hell, you crotchety old bag of feathers," Jeff muttered as he clicked on a lamp and confronted the raucous glee of the yellow-headed parrot in the tall wrought-iron cage. With deliberate care, he cut a small chunk of mango and flipped it through the bars into the feeding tray. Toulouse pounced on it immediately and devoured it with his sharp, hooked beak. Jeff systematically prepared the remaining fruit, tossed it, then threw in a few sunflower seeds for good measure. Then he flipped on the radio and sank into his chair.

But the cool tones of Count Basie weren't working their usual magic. Neither was the cold imported beer, or the suspense thriller in his lap. Jeff shifted in his burgundy leather recliner, seeking a position that would soothe the knots out of his system.

But such a position didn't exist on this night. He dragged his eyes away from the blurred print in front of him and stared instead into space. Unfortunately, that space was quickly replaced by slanting green eyes and frothy auburn curls, by a fragile weight he could still feel curled in his arms.

Cecil of the brilliant hair, brilliant eyes, brilliant smile. The years had softened her edges physically, sharpened them mentally. And the results were rather intriguing.

And then there were her kids.

He braced his wide hands on the arms of the chair and pushed off, a movement almost violent in its urgency. What had gotten into him?

Why couldn't he get her out of his head? His reaction to her wasn't logical, and was driving him crazy. The color-coordinated wardrobe hanging in his closet was practical. Running to keep his weight down was reasonable. Everything in his life was orderly. And that was precisely the way he liked it. Cecil was none of these things. In fact, she topped the list as the most impractical, unreasonable, disorderly woman he had ever known.

She said she didn't have room for him in her life? Well, that went double for him. Cecilia Evans in his life would be—"catastrophic" might be too mild a word. Besides, it was almost April. His work schedule was enough to drain the very life out of him, if he didn't love it so.

But if he loved it so, why wasn't he working on the Desmond account?

He plowed his fingers through his hair and braced himself against the terrace door, staring at the Dallas skyline, imagining the red Mobil Oil Pegasus that had been the skyline's trademark during his youth. Instead the green argon outline of the Interfirst Bank building blocked his view. It bothered him that the Mobil horse no longer flew above the city; now taller, newer buildings formed walls around it. You had to enter downtown from precisely the right angle to catch a glimpse of the winged horse.

But the horse flew still, if you knew where to find it.

The red neon horse reminded him a lot of his youth. Reminders of his youth were walled away from everyday perusal, dwarfed by the importance of his present, the excitement of his future. He hadn't bothered to attend any of his class reunions, to keep up with old classmates. Occasionally he'd see someone in a chance meeting. Their "where have you been?" would be followed by surprise that he'd been right here all along. Dallas was a big place. You could get lost in it with no problem.

Lost.

What a strange thought. He wasn't lost. It was this night, this melancholy mood that was depressing him.

It was Cecil.

He pivoted away from the view. Seventeen years ago he'd fantasized about strangling her. Tonight his fantasies were of an entirely different nature.

Suddenly it hit him how to get her out of his head. How to replace visions of tender, vulnerable lips with those of the big-mouthed brat she once had been. His jaw set with determination, he picked up his beer bottle from the glass-topped table and headed for the spare room. Cool, stale air met him when he entered, and he set his beer on the battered old upright piano. He opened the closet, flipped on the light and squatted to sort through the boxes of paraphernalia from his past.

In the third box, beneath a yellowed baccalaureate program and purple-and-gold tassels from his graduation cap, he found what he was looking for: his high school yearbooks. A cursory glance through the index, and then he found her name. *Greene, Cecilia*, followed by the four page numbers where her picture would be found.

The first was a group shot of her freshman homeroom class. Nothing inspiring there, except that she was in the center of the front row, with a short skirt that exposed a pair of nicely curved legs that had always been too curvey, too shapely, too perfect to belong to the likes of Cecilia Greene.

Pages 132 and 147 were more of the same—club pictures, too many people crammed into too small a space. Yet somehow his eyes went right to hers in each shot. That impish grin, pointed chin and eyes that seemed to be laughing at him still. Even in black and white, Cecil's vibrancy leaped right off the page.

His exercise in exorcism wasn't working at all.

She'd always been a cute kid, hadn't she? Funny that he'd never noticed it at the time. His fingers itched to tug one of those curls. Or maybe just to play in them, stroke them, feel them against his cheek....

"Play it, Sam!" A loud squawk sounded from the other end of the apartment. "She can take it, so can I!" The bird squawked again.

He slammed the yearbook closed in disgust.

Cecilia yanked the deep drawer out of the rolltop desk and lugged it to the breakfast table, sweeping the sports page of the newspaper to the floor to make room. She dug through the drawer's contents, groping for the leatherette zipper bag that held her bank statements. It would have made more sense to work at the desk, but she would have had to clean the blame thing off, which often took a couple of hours because she'd get sidetracked a half-dozen times.

It was the first Tuesday of the month. Sweet horseshoes, how she hated first Tuesdays. But putting them off had gotten her in trouble more than once, so she might as well make the best of it.

She reached in her jeans' back pocket and pulled out her checkbook, then she switched on the heavy, old calculator.

First she entered the amount of Robert's child support check in the checkbook. At least that was one worry she didn't have. Robert was a firm believer in electronic banking, and like clockwork, the money was deposited in her account each month. And like clockwork, half of it immediately got mailed to the mortgage company. She recorded these figures by heart.

Then, as a morale booster and conscience nudger, she examined her savings passbook and recent interest statements. The amount of money in the account would have boggled her mind two years ago when she had first faced a month of bills without Robert. She had been shy on money but long on determination.

She still derived pleasure from remembering the expression on Robert's face when she'd declined his assistance job hunting. She'd shunned the office jobs she was totally incapable of performing.

Actually singing for their supper made as much sense as anything else in her topsy-turvy world. Hadn't she put Robert through his last two years of engineering school by singing with Dallas's hottest local rock band? Of course, Dallas in the seventies hadn't exactly been the center of the musical world. The quality of the typical Dallas garage band in those days had been dismal indeed.

But Feather and the Falcons had been in great demand, performing at local night spots. She and Robert had lived on a shoestring. He studied while she worked; she slept while he attended classes. But somehow they'd managed to fill the remaining hours with some pretty decent memories. Things had been tight, but livable.

Now she consoled herself with the same words: tight, but livable—with one important difference. The first time around she had been saving for Robert's future, assuming she'd be part of it. This time, she was fighting for her own.

By her calculations, shaky though they might be, she figured she'd have a large enough nest egg in two more years to stop singing and enroll at the university full-time. If she worked hard, she could earn a degree in music education in three years and land a teaching job in time to help pay for Peter's college expenses. She tramped down the guilty feeling that she ought to be trying to take a few classes already. She simply couldn't handle any more right now.

As if to reassure her, Ralph lumbered over and dropped his big head onto her lap, sending several papers flitting to the floor. Cecilia scooped them up and was returning them to the table, when an envelope caught her eye. How had a check ended up with the bills?

She tore open the envelope. Money. The tightness in her chest eased a little. She ticked off the upcoming gigs on the calendar, the sure dates with Stan, the dates he'd given her cash in her hot, sweaty little hands. The commercial jingles were growing more frequent, but sometimes payment was slow.

But with this check for the Happy Haven Mobile Homes commercial, she'd ride easy for the month. Then her eyes lighted on the savings book. If she couldn't start school immediately, the least she could do was add to the nest egg.

"Well, which one of you guys is gonna scream the loudest if I don't pay you in full this month?" she asked the pile of still unopened bills.

Jeff tilted his leather swivel chair back and massaged the back of his neck. The sounds of movement from outside his office confirmed what his aching body was telling him. It was six o'clock. The stack of questionable tax forms McVay had left on his desk earlier that afternoon told him he was staying.

But taunting him from the corner of his polished walnut desk top was a small, scratched circle of glass. It had been there for two days, inviting him to throw it in the trash, tempting him to return it to its owner, or rather, its owner's mother.

He fingered the watch crystal, held it up and looked through it to the abstract print on the opposite wall. The symmetrical lines of varying widths of black, gray and red appeared asymmetrical, thanks to the scratches on the crystal. With a disgusted sigh he threw it into the trash can. Typical. Anything associated with Cecilia Evans was bound to distort his vision of a perfect and orderly world.

It was a cheap watch that could be easily and inexpensively replaced, anyway.

And the kid was a real pain in the neck. He hadn't even said thank-you. In fact, he'd told Jeff in no uncertain terms to stay away from his mother. As if Jeff needed any extra warning. Nope, Cecil brought him nothing but trouble. Always had, always would.

Trouble. In an attractive package, maybe. But trouble all the same.

Just thinking the words made him feel better. Relieved to have that nonsense out of his system, he reached for a file and pulled up a record on his computer. He input all of two figures before he shut it off again without saving the changes, and fished the watch crystal out of the trash can.

"Line up," Cecilia ordered.

"I can do it myself," Peter said.

"I know you can, but you didn't, so now I'm going to." She stifled further protests with a soapy washcloth applied firmly to his chin, determined to remove all evidence of Magic Marker. Finally satisfied, she thumbed him toward the sink. "You're next, Brad."

"But I already washed," he protested halfheartedly as the washcloth dove behind his ear. Forty-five seconds later, she aimed him toward the sink to rinse. Anne-Elizabeth, her TCU Horned Frog sweatshirt pulled up to her eyebrows, her arms locked firmly over her head, shouted a muffled "No" from behind the horned frog's lumpy belly.

Cecilia fought the urge to yank the sweatshirt down and teach her daughter who was boss. Instead she tickled her exposed belly button with the washcloth. Immediately arms and sweatshirt dropped and somehow, amidst the ensuing squealing frenzy, Cecilia washed her daughter's face passably clean. Next she ordered all three children into the living room and lined them up on the sofa, each on a separate cushion.

"No touching, no name-calling, no moving for the next five minutes while I get dressed, is that clear?" she directed, switching on the television for good measure.

Standing in the bathroom in her bra and half-slip, she heard the doorbell ring. "Nobody can play!" she called down the hall over the chorus of "I'll get its" that reverberated off the walls. She listened long enough to hear Peter order whoever it was away, then she shut the bathroom door. Humming, she experimented with a pair of tortoiseshell combs, trying to decide whether to pull her hair to one side in an avant garde twist, or simply sweep it out of her eyes in a more traditional "motherly" style. Her hum grew in volume until her vocalizing bounced off the walls, pure tones of a more classical nature than her usual style. It was the bathroom that always did it to her—the acoustics gave her voice a richness that tempted her to attempt Puccini instead of Manilow. She broke off in mid-warble; she'd better hurry.

When she emerged from the bathroom, her hair combed, teeth brushed and lips lined, she saw Jeff standing in the front doorway on the other side of the screen door.

"Cecil, is that you?"

"Eeek!" She ducked back into the bathroom and plastered her body against the door, her heart thumping a wild tatoo. Just exactly how dark was the hallway? She gulped, then thrust her head out. "Yes. What do you want?"

"I have something for you ... Peter wouldn't let me in." He sounded exasperated.

"Just a minute!" She scanned the bathroom for something to put on, then called, "Brad, will you come here a minute?" When his carrot top poked around the bathroom door, she hissed, "Bring me my dress. And my hose and my shoes, while you're at it!"

He returned with the red silk she had worn Saturday night.

"I meant the blue one!"

"This one was on the floor. I figured you were gonna wear it again, or else you'd've hung it up, right?" He managed to keep such an innocent expression on his face, she could almost pretend there wasn't a hidden barb in the eight-year-old's remark. Almost.

Cecilia dropped to the chaise lounge and began pulling her panty hose over her ankles. "The blue dress, Brad. And hurry."

Minutes later she strolled out of the bathroom looking, well, if not like a million bucks, somewhere close. Red silk would have been a million, but entirely inappropriate for a family excursion.

She walked to the door and she saw a mischievous sparkle in his eyes, the playful twist of his lips.

"Mom can't play ... what a shame."

Cecilia stopped short, her cheeks flaming. And when his eyes flickered down the front of her soft chambray dress, she had the distinct sensation he had more than an idle idea of what was beneath.

She pushed forward and unhooked the screen. "I'm sorry. I didn't realize they would take me so literally."

"Oh, it was deliberate I'm sure." He cast a sidelong glance into the living room, where Peter kept a studiously concentrated gaze on the flickering image of the television.

"We're on our way out." When he didn't respond, she prompted, "You said you had something for me?"

He grinned, the familiar dimples deepening, and slid his hand into his trouser pocket. He pulled out a small glass disk. "I believe this belongs to your eldest, er, child."

"I'm sure he'll be grateful," she murmured as he dropped it into her palm.

"I doubt it." He propped an elbow against the door frame, for all the world as though he were staking a claim. His jacket flared to expose his trim middle. "But it doesn't really make any difference. The watch crystal was just an excuse."

"An excuse?"

"For being here." His eyes teased her with sparkling gold pleasure. The interest in those glittering eyes was as pronounced as the glittering gold stickpin in his red silk tie. And it was an interest she was trying her darnedest not to reciprocate. Her palm felt oddly tingly where the watch crystal nestled, as if his touch lingered, radiating heat. She closed her fingers around it and thrust her fist into the pocket of her circular blue skirt, then glanced into the living room. Peter's eyes were trained on her, his expression hard.

"Thank you." It sounded lame enough, even to her ears, but what was she supposed to say, now go home?

She didn't have to.

"Where are you going, all dressed up?"

Remembering the rustle of red silk on the chaise in the bathroom, she shrugged. "Not dressed up. Not really." Then realizing she hadn't answered his question, she added, "To school. Tonight's open house. Texas Public Schools Week."

"Open house? Good grief, I haven't been to an open house since I was a kid." Jeff tilted his head, a slanting ray of late evening sun catching the lean angles of his face. His skin was a warm tan. Not tanned by the sun, because Cecilia would venture a guess that he hadn't spent a measurable amount of time in the sun in years. And not olive, because olive tended to sallow in the winter. Just a warm, natural shade of brown.

"Cecil, in case you're being a little dense, I just dropped a big hint."

"Hint?" she choked out, hoping he hadn't noticed her scrutiny.

He took her by the arm and led her deeper into the hall, out of range of the living room. "I realize you've been out of circulation awhile, so I'll refresh your memory. I said 'I haven't been to an open house in years,' to which you could have replied, 'Well, why don't you come with us?'"

"What?" she gasped. "You? At the school?"

"Why such surprise?" he asked, edging a little closer. He stroked her cheekbone with his knuckle, blazing a tingling trail along her jaw and down her neck.

"Mom." Peter stood framed in the doorway, staring. "If we're not going to school tonight, just say so."

"We are going. Mr. Smith is leav—"

"Agreeing to go with you," Jeff inserted smoothly. He confronted Peter's stare without flinching, then straightened his wide shoulders and tightened his jaw. Propelling Cecilia forward, he added, "Your mother was kind enough to invite me. I hope you don't find that a problem."

Peter's sullen gaze swept from Jeff to his mother and back to Jeff again. Without a word, he spun away and pushed through the screen door, letting it slam behind him, which was a totally un-Peterish thing to do. Hearing the commotion, Brad dashed after him. *Slam.*

Anne-Elizabeth brought up the rear.

Slam.

"Excuse me," Cecilia grated, "while we have a family conference."

She cornered the children on the front walk. The conference was brief and explicit. Peter's expression was sullen, but he didn't argue. Cecilia ordered them into the Suburban, then returned to the porch where Jeff was waiting, his expression quizzical. "Who won?"

"Jeff," Cecilia apologized, "I don't think that will happen again."

"Door slamming?"

"Oh, good grief, no." She laughed in spite of herself. "This door doesn't remember how to shut without slamming. I just don't think Peter will..." Will what? Peter was not likely to hide his feelings for long. "I don't think he'll be quite so...blatant." She smiled weakly. "At least not tonight."

Jeff cocked his head and smiled. "How far is it to the school?"

"About four blocks," she said. "But you're not going."

"Of course I am. I am totally intrigued by the prospects of salt maps, tissue paper bluebonnets and sugar cube Alamos." His wry chuckle belied his words charmingly.

"But why? Why on earth do you want to go?"

"I don't. Not really." He grinned, and she couldn't tear her gaze away. "But if it means I can follow you around, watch your hips sway and fantasize about your raspberry underwear..."

"What?" Cecilia stepped away from him, her heart thudding the rhythm of a panic-stricken hare when the fox has just entered the back door. "You—you saw!"

Jeff nudged her toward the door. "Hurry up and lock the door, Cecil. The kids are waiting."

Two hours later, Cecilia and Jeff sat side by side on her front porch swing, eating ice cream, while the kids shared theirs with Vinny and Mikey and Ralph in the backyard. With his shirt-sleeves rolled back, exposing the dark hair on his forearms, his hair ruffled from the breeze, Jeff once again had changed before her eyes.

"I really don't know what I'm going to do with you, Jefferson Smith."

"Every time you 'Jefferson Smith' me that way, I know I'm in for it."

"Saturday morning you told me in no uncertain terms that you thought I had problems, then when you picked up your car you acted as if I had a contagious disease."

"Is that the way you remember it?"

"All right," she said, relenting. "I wasn't exactly cordial, I'll admit. But doesn't that show you we really don't get along very well?"

"You might say that," he agreed, seemingly more interested in his double dip chocolate cone than her.

"Don't drip," she commanded as the soft edge of his chocolate ice cream threatened to dribble onto his trousers.

He caught the drip on his tongue, avoiding her eyes. "Did I mention that I promised Brad I'd photograph his soccer game this weekend?"

"You're going to his soccer game?" she repeated numbly.

"I'd like to try some action shots on some new film I'm testing, and this seems as good an opportunity as I'll get."

She angled herself toward him on the porch swing. "What exactly are you trying to prove? You just admitted that you and I don't get along at all, so why don't you leave well enough alone? Leave *me* alone?"

"Do you honestly want me to leave you alone, Cecil?"

Five days earlier, the answer would have been a desperate and resounding yes. Four days earlier, more desperate if less resounding, but still yes. But tonight, she was churning with emotions ranging from exasperation and frustration to a tingling awareness she couldn't deny. The word "yes" wouldn't form on her lips.

What if he did walk away? Never called again. Never crossed her threshold again. Disappeared from her life as completely as the first time. Where was the sense of relief she ought to feel? Surely it was still there, somehow camouflaged by the emptiness that threatened to overwhelm her. She turned blindly to her ice-cream cone. She couldn't answer him.

Nervously she wiped a smudge of raspberry sherbert from the tip of her nose.

"I wish I had gotten raspberry."

"There's plenty more," she said, seizing any excuse to break the tension between them. "Do you want me to fix you one?"

He shifted his weight and eased closer to her. His deep brown eyes darkened dreamily beneath half-closed lids. "Don't get up," he murmured. "I'll just have a taste of yours...."

She knew she should turn away from his lips, but she didn't. She could have at least given him a moving target. But she didn't. And when his lips hesitated a mere breath away from hers, and she knew what was coming, and even knew that she wanted it, she could have, *should* have at least closed her eyes and waited.

But she didn't.

Instead she closed the gap and touched her lips to his. She'd waited seventeen years for this kiss, and she'd be damned if she was going to turn away from it now.

At first they were joined only by that basic union, her lips soft and tentative, his cautious and exploring. After a moment's gentle awakening, they melted together inch by inch, until she couldn't tell where she stopped and he began as her curves yielded to his hard angles.

Her lips parted and she felt the warm velvet sweep of his tongue tracing her lips with growing intensity, the chocolate and raspberry flavors blending ever so sweetly. She shivered at the delicious sensations his gently probing kiss brought to life. Everything was happening so slowly, so deliberately, it seemed an eternity before her raspberry cone dropped onto the porch with a plop, followed by its chocolate counterpart.

Her hand sought his thick, wavy hair, and she pulled his head firmly to hers, shuddering as she felt his fingers inching down her body in exploration. Finally his hands rested on her slender waist. His thumbs slid the soft cotton fabric against her ribcage, circling ever upward until they were brushing the lower curves of her breasts with a tantalizing, erotic rhythm. She moaned softly into his mouth, pulling slightly away from his body to allow his hands more freedom to move. She gasped when his thumbs found the hard imprint of her nipples, felt a heat spreading when his low groan revealed his response was as great as her own.

Sensations assaulted her one after another, his taste on her lips, the faint smell of his cologne, the sound of his shirt rasping against her dress, the feel of his hands cupping her softness, then kneading in slow, deliberate movements.

Oh, yes, this was something she could get used to very quickly.

He chose that moment to pull away.

She took three deep, agonizingly slow breaths, before she muttered a raspy, "Oh, my."

Even Jeff sounded a little strained as he rested his head against the creaking chain. "'Oh, my?' Is that the best you can do?"

"I . . . I just can't help remembering . . ."

"Remembering what?"

"How I yearned, how I plotted, how I fantasized about kissing you." She turned a startled face to him. "Good grief, I don't think I would have survived it at fourteen!"

His voice amused, Jeff added, "And to think I ran from it."

He placed a finger under her chin and tilted her face up to his. Even in the darkness, she felt the intensity of his gaze boring into her. "I wonder now, what would you have done with me if you had caught me?"

"Oh, Lord," she whispered, her eyes large and frightened.

"I know exactly what I'd do with you if I caught—"

"No, you don't!" She pushed at his chest. "You can just forget that right now. I don't have time for your games, whatever they are. I'm a mother—"

"I know."

"With children and responsibilities—"

"I noticed."

"And I've changed. So let's forget this ever happened." She struck his chest for emphasis. "Do you hear me?" He refused to answer, only smiled that slow smile she had to steel herself against.

His mouth sought hers once again, but she twisted away. "I'm not fourteen now, and I'm not chasing you. What's more, I'm not interested in being chased, or seduced, or whatever you want to call it."

"You sure talk a lot, kid," he murmured, finally letting her go. And then added with a wicked grin, "I'm beginning to see exactly how much fun chasing can be."

Cecilia leaped to her feet. The swing careened wildly as he stood, as well. "I mean it, Jefferson Smith! I'm going to go into the house, put my children to bed and forget that you made a pass at me. I'm not interested! Is that clear?" She strode to the door and had her hand on the handle, when Jeff joined her.

"Go right ahead with your exciting evening." He pressed his palm against the door; she pulled but couldn't budge it. "But as for forgetting what just happened between us..." He raked her body with his eyes before planting one last, lingering kiss on her forehead.

"You can try."

Five

The children had been asleep for hours. The wind was picking up; a cold front must be coming through. An occasional gust caught the swing and sent it creaking; it slowed and quieted; another gust, and the creaking started again.

Cecilia raised up on one elbow and studied the digital clock across the room: midnight. The witching hour. And she'd be a witch tomorrow unless she got some sleep. Her shoulders ached from tossing from one side to the other, and her neck was getting stiff.

This is ridiculous. She switched on the radio, sat upright in the bed and folded her arms across her knees. Resting her cheek on her arms, she stared out the window.

"Midnight Express...golden oldies..." droned the late night deejay in sultry tones. The coarse, grating squeal of an electric guitar coupled with the baroque pattern of an organ keyboard pierced her mind. The song had never been one of her favorites; she'd always wanted lyrics to sing along with.

Still, on this night, with the half-bare tree limbs undulating in an eerie dance, the music seemed appropriate, oddly reminiscent of a distant era of her life. Yet the past was haunting her like a ghost. Closing her eyes, she could almost smell the incense and see the black-light fluorescence splashing across the visions of her subconscious.

Memories tugged at her, pulled her back to her high school years. And of course, those had begun with ... with a freshman girl tripping over a senior boy and sprawling, geeklike, at his feet.

He was the last thing she wanted to think about now. His sudden return into her life was keeping her awake in the first place.

And, of course, those memories also included Robert.

No, the past held no solace for a sleepless night.

She slipped into her terry robe and padded through the house to the kitchen. Dreading the blinding ceiling light, she used the diffused glow from the light above the stove to see. On the top shelf of the corner cabinet she found what she wanted: a dusty bottle of wine that had been waiting for a celebration for two and a half years. A gift from a well-meaning friend after her divorce. Somehow Cecilia had never thought of the divorce as something to commemorate with Chablis.

So tonight it would serve a far more useful purpose: calm her frazzled nerves and help her sleep. She had two recording sessions tomorrow, nine to twelve at Ad-Com, Inc., and one to four at RPM Productions. A wine-filled juice glass cupped in her hand, she grimaced. Had she remembered to find a place for the kids after school?

It was funny how wide-awake she had felt in bed, and how tired she felt now that she was on her feet. A steady scraping noise drew her to the living room window. She pulled back the lace curtains and peered into the yard. The pecan trees needed trimming again. Every three years Robert climbed up with a chain saw and cut the branches away from the house. This must be the third year, and Robert wasn't here to do it. She pictured herself on the highest limb with the roaring chainsaw and had to stifle a giggle. She supposed she'd have to hire someone. Damn. She certainly didn't want to see her money go out for such mundane things as tree trimming. Maybe Jeff...

Don't be ridiculous, she scolded herself, and pivoted away from the window, inadvertently splashing the cool wine down her neck. It tickled down the valley between her breasts, and she dabbed at it with a corner of her robe. One way or another Jeff kept her awake, and she didn't have time for such nonsense.

She tipped the glass to her lips and drained it, determined to sleep at all costs. But her sleep was haunted all night by his lips, his eyes, his gently taunting laugh....

In the car, with the windows rolled up tight and the music blaring, Cecilia warmed up her voice. She parked in the shadow of the skyscrapers and dashed seven blocks to the recording studio near downtown Dallas. Breathless, she rushed into the building at 9:02.

"Lookin' good, darlin'," came a peppy male voice. Mitch Delaney, Stan Delaney's nephew, motioned to her from across the marble-floored lobby.

"Hi, Mitch."

Short of stature and stout like his bandleader uncle, the younger Delaney was a music student at SMU. He sometimes played trumpet in the band when his uncle needed someone on short notice, and he also worked as a studio musician for Ad-Com and some of the other production companies in town.

She hardly slowed for him to catch up with her. "I'm running late. I can't talk." As she hurried to the elevator, he fell in step beside her.

"Take it easy. There's a big pileup on Stemmons Freeway and Karla's bound to be stuck in the middle of it. You're safe."

"Thank goodness." She sighed, the tension in her shoulders loosening.

"Rough night?" he asked as the elevator doors shut them into a Muzak-filled cocoon.

She leaned against the walnut-paneled wall and nodded. "But I'm here. That's the main thing."

"I hope you're in good voice."

Something in his tone clued her that the remark was not idle chitchat. "What's up?"

"Dondi Cramer got called out of town. Family problems."

Cecilia's pulse raced. "Too bad. Hope it's nothing serious."

"Serious enough to keep her in Michigan for a week or two."

Muted bells binged as they passed one floor after the other in silence. Mitch was doing her a big favor by letting her know about Dondi's absence. Dondi was one of the elite, one of the dozen or so singers in Dallas who got the majority of radio-jingle work in the city—no small feat, as Dallas was known in the industry as the "commercial jingle capital" of the nation. Cecilia had filled in on rare occasions when one or another of the female singers was unavailable. But if Dondi was going to be out for over a week... Her palms itched just thinking about it. Dondi's absence might give Cecilia a chance at more jobs, more money, and boy, did she need it.

The doors opened, and Cecilia and Mitch stepped into the swank and savvy waiting room of Ad-Com, Inc. Cecilia passed through the mauve-and-gray room with scarcely a glance, her mind racing. Should she play it dumb and just sing her heart out, or take the bull by the horns and ask up front for Dondi's work?

She was about to turn into the hallway to the studio, when Mitch called to her.

"Cecilia, has Uncle Stan talked to you about the April 1 gig yet?"

She halted in midstride. April 1. She turned slowly. "I don't know anything about it."

"The podiatrists' convention."

She shook her head. "What's up?"

Mitch's face crinkled into a double-chinned grin. "Uncle Stan and Aunt Marge are going out of town that weekend for their thirtieth anniversary, you know. I'm leading the band for him so he won't have to back out of the convention. I'll get back with you later about a few ideas I have."

"Sure, sure." Cecilia nodded impatiently, then pushed through the double doors to the studio.

To her chagrin, Karla was waiting for her, clipboard and frown in place. The large clock on the wall behind the producer read an accusing 9:07.

Cecilia grabbed a set of headphones and headed for the mike. No time for bullfighting, she decided quickly. Karla handed her a sheet of music and headed for the control booth. The taped background, a gentle twang of country guitar, played into her ears, and Cecilia hummed along as she read the music. Two takes later she felt the appropriate huskiness in her voice, the right "catch" when she slid into the upper register. "'K-Shine on my shoulder makes me happy...'" Karla nodded her approval and put on another spot.

Cecilia sailed through the morning in record time, completing several variations of three different spots, one country, one upbeat pop and one "plain vanilla" for an all-news station in Eugene, Oregon. The different spots were sent to customer stations all over the U.S. The voice-overs were added later by one of the client stations' deejays.

Cecilia was reapplying her lipstick, using the glass window of the control booth as a mirror, when Karla stepped out and approached her. "How are you for Friday morning and all next Tuesday and Wednesday? Wednesday may be a late session. I have a hole to fill, and I think you might work."

Cecilia made a show of pulling her agenda out of her shoulder bag, an act that probably didn't fool Karla one bit. She flipped it open, studied it a minute, then her face fell. "Friday's fine, and so is Tuesday...." She forced a smile. "I can make it Wednesday, too."

"Be on time," Karla warned, and headed back to the control booth.

Cecilia wrote the new sessions on the small calendar, but her hand paused at the 6:00 soccer game penciled in for Wednesday. Then, squelching her guilt, she marked Wednesday for Ad-Com and snapped the book shut. Somehow she'd figure something out.

In the meantime, she'd see if Dondi Cramer had left any holes at RPM that Cecilia Evans might conveniently fill.

* * *

The alarm tone pulsed relentlessly until Jeff finally hit the right button and shut it off. He squinted up at the ceiling, his eyes aching from too many long hours staring at spread sheets on a computer screen. He stretched, yawned, rubbed his eyes and breathed a contented sigh. The last thing he wanted to do on this Saturday morning was drag himself out of bed, much less spend the day in the bright Texas sun.

He sure as hell didn't want to go to that blasted soccer game. He rolled over, pulled the pillow over his head and prepared to dig back into some serious sleep time.

The alarm sounded again. He had hit the Snooze instead of the Off button. He slammed his hand down, hitting several buttons at once, and pulled the pillow tighter over his head. Sleep. Pure and simple, it was all he wanted, all he needed.

A muffled screech came down the hall. Too damn bad, he thought rebelliously. Let the bird wait for his food; it wouldn't kill him. He sank deeper into the covers. No luxury compared to stealing extra sleep in the middle of the busiest tax season in memory....

Whatever had Cecil done about hers? Visions of Cecilia Greene Evans hauled into tax court and then to jail ricocheted through his mind. And she deserved it, too, the way she and that obnoxious kid of hers thought they could handle the Tax Bill of 1986.

Toulouse squawked, Jeff clenched his teeth, and sleep slid from his grasp. He rolled over and kicked the covers off his legs. Old habits break hard, and he'd gotten up early too many days for too many consecutive weeks.

With Toulouse perched on his shoulder, smelling of banana and chattering meaninglessly, Jeff downed a quick glass of juice.

"Bang, bang!" the bird squawked.

Jeff tried to ignore him as he pulled a pair of khaki shorts out of his drawer.

"Bang, bang!" Toulouse tightened his talons, and Jeff winced and cursed, and gave in.

After pulling on his shorts he took the parrot to his perch in the living room, paced five steps away, whirled, aimed a forefinger and shouted, "Bang!"

Toulouse screamed and fell backward, wings outspread and hung suspended upside down, a "death" worthy of an Emmy at the very least. Jeff laughed in spite of himself. "You mangy old bird," he grumbled.

Toulouse righted himself on the perch and edged back and forth in excitement. "Bang, bang! Bang, bang!"

Jeff "killed him" four more times to assuage his own guilt. Toulouse wasn't going to be happy when he put him back in the cage. But after all, Jeff had promised the kid he'd take pictures, and he remembered all too well how broken promises hurt an eight-year-old boy.

For ten minutes Jeff wandered aimlessly between the soccer fields, his tripod in one hand, his photo equipment still in his shoulder bag; the sheer numbers of bouncing, dribbling, squealing, screaming, racing, colliding children left him awestruck. He was about to turn tail and run, when he saw Cecilia. She saw him at the same time. Her face lit up, first in surprise, then pleasure, then quickly slid into a frown.

"I didn't think you were coming," she said irritably.

The frown didn't fool him; he chose to dwell on the pleasure. "But you were hoping?"

Her flush told him he was right on target. "I wouldn't have missed it for the world." The fib didn't bother him as he fell into step beside her. "How many fields are there?"

"Twelve," she responded.

"Looks like a thousand kids out here."

"This must be a real cultural shock for you since you're not around kids much."

"Try 'never,'" he said, laughing. "And I've never seen a soccer game before, either." He shifted his camera case to his other shoulder and edged closer to her.

When Cecilia sidestepped and widened the distance between them again, he smiled. Playing games with her was going to be more fun than soccer.

"Where are the kids?"

"Already at Brad's field. They ran on ahead. I'm too old to run."

"I guess I missed Peter's game," Jeff said, attempting to sound regretful.

He could tell by her sniff that she wasn't fooled. "It was a good game. They're the team everyone else tries to beat. Peter loves it, of course. Loves being superior, I mean."

"That doesn't surprise me," Jeff said. "How about Brad and his team?" She always seemed at ease when they talked about her kids. And if he had to discuss the little barbarians to improve her attitude, at least let it be about the one that was halfway human. He tried to concentrate on what she was saying, rather than the way the sun brightened her eyes and bounced glints of fire and gold off of her windtangled hair.

"Is the pits. We're talking major-league lousy. Hey, are you listening to me?"

"Yeah, sure."

"Well, like I was saying, no matter what happens, you can be sure the Bandits will flub it." She swept a spray of hair out of her eyes, then reached into her shoulder bag and pulled out an oversize pair of dark sunglasses.

No, he begged silently. Don't cover up your eyes.

But she perched them on her nose, half hiding her face from his eyes. "It's nobody's fault," she continued, scuffing the toes of her dingy yellow sneakers through the rough grass. "Individually they have some pretty good players." She flashed him a smile. "Brad's the best."

Realizing she was waiting for him to respond, Jeff waved toward the smaller field where the little boys were warming up in their red-white-and-blue uniforms. "Isn't losing so often tough on them?"

She straightened her shoulders almost imperceptibly and lifted her chin. "We parents don't let it. As long as they're having fun and learning the game, they're winners." Sheepishly she added, "Even if they have lost every game for the past two and a half seasons."

"Well, at least they have bright uniforms." Jeff raised his camera to catch Brad in action, but as he snapped the shutter, the boy saw him and stopped to wave. "I always did like red, white and blue,'' Jeff said as Brad scampered toward his team. ''Kind of makes you want to salute.''

Cecilia laughed with a huskiness that made him stop and look at her, but her full attention was trained on the boys. ''Believe it or not, at this age the uniform is almost the most important thing to those kids.''

''And what's the most important?''

''The cold drinks at the end of the game.'' She laughed again. If she'd take off those god-awful sunglasses so he could see her eyes ... If he could snap a picture of her like this, relaxed and laughing, instead of bristling. As a matter of fact, he wouldn't mind having a picture of her bristling, either. Or pensive. Or sleeping....

Whoa, he thought. Better snap out of it before he forgot who he'd come to photograph. He trotted down the field to get a better view of the game.

Time enough to deal with Cecil later. And deal with her, he would. With pleasure.

When the the game ended, the Bandits lined up to shake hands with their winning opponents, then stampeded off the field toward the cold drinks with more speed than they'd shown during the game.

''I still say if we put the ice chest behind the net, they'd score a lot more goals,'' Cecilia announced to general laughter. She gathered up her bag and Brad's discarded jersey while the coach announced the next practice.

''Didja get a picture of me headin' the ball?'' Brad asked as they started toward the parking lot. ''I did it twice.''

'' 'Heading'?'' Jeff queried.

''Yeah, you know.'' Brad tossed his soccer ball in the air, ran under it and let it bounce off his head before catching it. ''Headin' it.''

''Oh, sure.'' Jeff nodded. ''I think I may have gotten one. Here, want to carry this for me?''

Brad ducked under the camera strap and fell into step beside Jeff. The camera bounced off the boy's thighs with each step.

''When's that jerk goin' home, Mom?'' Peter demanded.

"Yeah, he's a jerk," Anne-Elizabeth echoed her elder brother.

"Both of you cut it out right now," Cecilia said sharply. "I don't want to hear any more of this 'jerk' business. Is that clear?"

Anne-Elizabeth looked to Peter for her response. Peter didn't answer at all, just kicked the soccer ball meticulously down the sideline of the field, his head ducked.

By the time they reached the cars, Brad and Jeff had already loaded the equipment into the convertible and had put the top down. "Mom," Brad called. "Jeff said I can ride in his car. You let Peter the other day, so now it's my turn, right?"

"Are you sure it's all right, Jeff?" Cecilia asked, her key poised at the door lock.

"Certainly."

With that, they climbed into the convertible and zoomed away, Brad waving just before they rounded the corner out of sight.

"Mom, can we get hamburgers to take home?" Peter asked as they passed a drive-thru hamburger restaurant. "Please?"

"I don't wanna hamburger," Anne-Elizabeth chimed in from the back seat. "I wanna jerk-burger!" she squealed.

When they pulled into the driveway, loaded down with malts, burgers and fries, they found Jeff and Brad already eating hamburgers on the porch swing. "You could at least have waited for us," Cecilia called out.

"What? And let our food get cold?" Jeff answered, washing down his food with a gulp of his drink.

"I hope everybody's hungry, because we bought lunch, too." Cecilia plopped down on the top porch step and began digging for Anne-Elizabeth's junior burger. "If I had known you wanted a picnic, we could have at least gone to the park."

"Oh, I kind of like eating on your porch swing. Want to join me?"

"No, thank you," she responded demurely, passing hamburgers out to grabbing hands.

They had nearly finished eating, when a black Mercedes pulled into the driveway. Cecilia paused, her hamburger suspended in transit to her mouth. Robert hadn't said anything about coming today, and especially not with Monica.

Monica emerged from the car and took Robert's arm. Her blond hair was sleeked back into a chignon, though a fluffy fringe of bangs flirted over her forehead, and her tailored wool slacks and silk blouse complemented her slender frame to perfection. In tan shorts and a green T-shirt, her hair windblown, her nose windburned to match her hair, Cecilia felt like a frump.

The couple walked toward them, hands entwined. "We just picked up our new car, and we thought the boys might like a joy ride," he said, pushing his free hand through his hair in a nervous gesture Cecilia remembered well. His smooth forehead creased in hard lines as he nodded at Jeff.

Jeff rose, wiped his hand on the seat of his shorts and took Robert's hand. Cecilia's gaze swung from one man to the other. Jeff seemed unaffected by the awkwardness of the situation, while Robert's eyes showed blue ice.

"This is really a surprise. It's been a long time, Jeff."

"Yeah, it has. Nice car you've got there."

"That's quite a beauty you have, too." Robert glanced at the T-Bird. "Brad's been telling me all about it."

Cecilia gulped. What else had Brad been saying? She realized she should say something, but for the life of her couldn't figure out what. She glanced from the two men towering over her to the half-eaten hamburger in her hand. "Y'all want a hamburger?" She lifted the sack of leftover burgers.

"No, honey. We've already eaten." Monica answered in dulcet tones. She cast an appraising look in Jeff's direction. "Isn't anyone going to introduce us?"

Robert made the introduction, and Cecilia noticed his discomfort when Monica purred her greeting to Jeff. Jeff smiled openly in response, his dark eyes twinkling.

Robert's hand closed possessively over Monica's upper arm. "Well, kids, do you want to take a ride?"

The children turned in unison to their mother. She saw their lack of enthusiasm about his offer, and knew that

Robert must have, too. "Run along and have fun." As they took off for the Mercedes, she added, "And behave yourselves!"

They were piling into the back seat, when she leaped to her feet, scattering French fries everywhere. "Robert, Anne-Elizabeth is filthy! She's been playing in the dirt all day. She'll ruin your upholstery."

"Don't worry," Monica cooed through her open window. "It's leather. It'll brush right off. You know how practical Robert is."

"Oh, yes, I certainly do." Cecilia smiled grimly and watched the "practical" Mercedes pull away from her eight-year-old Suburban. Anne-Elizabeth's bright, coppery head bobbed in the back window. "Buckle her up, you idiot," she muttered. There was a dull ache gnawing at her, and she didn't care to examine it.

"That guy sure knows how to pick 'em," Jeff murmured.

"Cars or women?" she retorted, kicking French fries off the steps and into the flower bed.

"Lemons." Jeff grinned and pulled her into his arms. "A connoisseur would never mistake flash and dazzle for real class." He cupped her chin and his fingers traced a delicate pattern on her cheek. "The guy's a jerk," he muttered as he lowered his lips to hers.

Cecilia's lips quivered beneath his, and tiny whimpering sounds escaped her. He lifted his head. "That's not exactly the response I've come to expect," he complained.

"I spent my youth falling for jerks, didn't I?" She collapsed against him as laughter overwhelmed her.

"You're not going bonkers on me, are you?" Jeff asked Cecilia cautiously. "'Cause I really did have some ideas about how to spend an afternoon without the Marx Brothers."

Cecilia was suddenly aware of his hard body against hers, aware of the too casual way she'd fallen into his arms. She broke away, both relieved and disappointed when he made no move to stop her. "Ideas? What kind of ideas?"

"Well, for starters, I think we should go inside. For a lady who is overly concerned about what the neighbors think, you sure do like to neck on the front porch."

"Me?" Cecilia straightened to her full height. "I beg your pardon!"

"Pardon granted, ma'am. Now what are we going to do with all these hamburgers?"

Cecilia looked at the littered porch and sighed. "Ralph is going to love us for this." She began scooping bags into her arms, Jeff following suit by picking up the scraps she missed. Her arms were full, when she remembered the key. "Darn."

"What's the problem, kid?"

"I stuck my keys in my back pocket." She bent over to unload her arms.

"Allow me," he said with a twinkle in his eye, and she felt his fingers inching into her pocket.

"Haven't you found them yet?" she asked, elbowing him in the stomach for good measure.

"Oh, yeah," he breathed huskily into her ear. "I found them." Slowly his hand slipped out of her pocket, and the keys jangled softly. "Why don't we go inside?"

She unlocked the door, her heart beating erratically.

"Do you remember painting 'JUST MARRIED' on my car the night of my senior prom?" Jeff asked as he patiently unloaded her arms, dropping the bags unheeded onto the floor.

"Er, I'm not sure I want to admit it," she muttered.

"My date thought I did it."

"As a joke?"

"As a proposal."

"You're kidding!"

Jeff shoved the bags aside with his foot. "Do you remember driving into the dead end where I was necking with Janice Youngblood, and you with flashing red lights on top of your father's car?"

"Really, Jeff, do we have to rehash all this ancient history?"

"Janice got a black eye when she banged into the steering wheel, and I slammed the car door on my foot trying to get out of there."

"Jeff, what exactly were you doing in that car?" she asked, fascinated in spite of herself.

"None of your business." Slowly, deliberately, he locked the front door. "I've just been thinking. You chased me so hard, so long." He smiled his lazy grin. "I think that it's time you caught me."

Six

Cecilia backed away from him until her heels bumped the bottom stair. "I don't like the look in your eye."

She took the stair blindly, refusing to consider whether she was stepping back to put more distance between them or stepping higher to close that distance.

She accomplished the latter.

"Really, Cecilia?" He moved closer, leaned closer, and didn't have so far to lean, so far to reach, as he lowered his head to tease her tense lips. "You don't like it?"

"I...er...no," she lied weakly. And then, inhaling deeply, she whispered, "Yes."

His arms closed around her and she felt herself melting, sliding backward, downward, until her hips settled on the stairs. Slowly she and Jeff leaned backward until they reclined, side by side, on the musty carpeted stairs. But along with the scent of dust, she breathed in the cool, outdoor fragrance of his skin, the sweet, clean scent of his sunwarmed cheek as he nuzzled her neck.

"Jeff..."

"I know," he murmured. "Hush, I know...." His mouth caressed hers as his hands moved gently over her body.

"This is crazy. We hardly know each other...really," she whispered, her fingers playing down the rippling muscles of his back as he moved over her.

"If half a lifetime isn't enough for you, it'll be a long time before you find someone you know any better, Cecil."

"That's not what I mean."

His face clouded. "This really is crazy, isn't it? I'm trying to talk you into something I don't even want myself."

"You don't?" She tried to keep the stab of disappointment from registering in her expression, her tone.

"I have no business being here in the first place. I have a stack of accounts I should be working on.... And yet, here I am. You explain it."

Cecilia opened her mouth to speak.

"Better yet, don't."

His lips captured hers, blocking the flow of her words. Just as well, she thought languidly as his hands slipped beneath her T-shirt. How could she explain his dilemma, when she was drowning in her own? She felt a quaking response to his touch that was the most intimate, dangerous of threats. All thoughts of "shouldn't" drained from her body. She sighed, that quietest of assents, and met the stroke of his tongue with the tip of her own, felt him react with a shudder, then felt the last barriers fall from between them as her breasts swelled into his palms. The movements of his hard body demanded, and she responded, past questioning.

The roar of the Mercedes motor rumbled into her consciousness.

She groaned in frustration. "They're back."

Angry voices, children's voices, sliced between them, and he pulled away, his eyes dark with confusion and frustration.

A car door slammed, then another, and the voices came nearer. Cecilia pulled down her shirt as Jeff sat up straight on the stairs, his face flushed.

"Smooth your hair," she hissed, trying to fluff her own into place.

The doorbell rang, and rang again, as the kids pounded on the door. "I'm coming," she called, gesturing wildly at Jeff until he got up and crossed into the living room, where

he fell back onto the love seat in a semblance of noncha-
lance.

"That was a short trip," she said brightly, but her attempted smile vanished when she saw Peter's strained
expression and Brad and Anne-Elizabeth's tearstained faces.
Robert loomed behind them, obviously enraged.

"What's wrong?" Cecilia demanded.

"Is this the way they behave when I'm not around to
handle things?" he demanded. "Can't you control these
kids?"

The hairs on the back of her neck bristled with anger.
"What do you mean? You were the one who was with
them," she snapped. "What happened?"

"I'll talk to you later. I need to go to Monica—she's very
upset."

"She's not the only one who's upset. Haven't you taken
a good look at your children?" She motioned them into the
house.

"Look," Jeff interceded smoothly, sauntering up behind her. "This isn't the time or place for this, Cecil. Why
don't you two talk this over when you've calmed down a
little?"

"That's an excellent idea, though it really doesn't concern you, Smith," Robert snapped. "When you quit being
so defensive, *Cecilia*, maybe we can discuss this like adults."

"Discuss *what*?" She clenched her fists at her sides, but
Jeff's hand on her elbow gave her the strength to control her
fury. "Go take care of Monica. I'll take care of the children."

After she shoved the door shut, she collapsed against it
and faced the kids.

"Let's get to the bottom of this right now," Cecilia commanded, pointing them toward the living room. Her temples throbbing, she lined up the children in front of her. Jeff
retreated to the love seat again.

They looked at her from large, frightened eyes. Belat-
edly, she realized that they must think her rage was directed
at them. "What happened?" she asked in a softer tone of
voice.

"Anne-Elizabeth bit Monica," Peter answered without hesitation.

"She did *what*?" She stared at the three of them incredulously.

"She bit her—she really did," Brad offered helpfully.

"Annie," she gasped softly, "did you bite Monica?" Please let this be some kind of mistake, she begged silently.

"She called me names, Mommy." Her eyes pleaded for understanding, but her tiny body didn't move.

"Before or after you bit her?"

"Mostly after," Peter conceded when Anne-Elizabeth refused to answer.

"I see," Cecilia said, though she really didn't. Deciding that her daughter wasn't going to be much help, she turned to Brad and Peter. "Okay, why did she bite her?"

"Monica was kissin' Daddy," Brad answered, his eyes downcast. "Daddy stopped at a red light, and she leaned over and kissed him, and the next thing we knew, Anne-Elizabeth had bitten a hunk out of her arm."

"My God," Jeff muttered.

"A hunk?" Cecilia asked, feeling a little sick to her stomach.

"No," Peter corrected impatiently. "She just bled a little, that's all."

Cecilia stared mutely at her children, who were all visibly shaken by the episode. "Okay, kids. This is pretty awful. Give me time to think about it."

They nodded, relieved.

"There are a lot of hamburgers and French fries in the hall. Brad, Peter, why don't you take them outside and feed Ralph?" The two older boys beat a hasty retreat.

"Sweetheart, I know this is hard for you to understand," Cecilia said, measuring and stressing each word, "but Monica can kiss Daddy if she wants to."

"She's not my mommy." Her full lower lip extended into a tremulous pout.

"I know she's not, honey." Cecilia grasped for an explanation she'd understand. "But she is Daddy's wife. And she can kiss him, and he can kiss her because they're married to each other. Do you understand?"

"They mawwied to each other," she muttered, not meeting Cecilia's eyes.

"And they can kiss each other," Cecilia coached.

"And they can kiss each other," Anne-Elizabeth repeated through trembling lips.

"You didn't understand that, and that's why you bit her, right?"

"Yeah."

"And you're sorry you bit her, aren't you?"

Silence.

Cecilia decided to change tactics. "You love Daddy, don't you?"

The small, tousled head nodded hesitantly.

"Well, Daddy loves Monica. And if you love Daddy, you'll be nice to Monica."

More silence.

"Anne-Elizabeth, are you going to bite Monica again?" Cecilia asked, a trace of threat in her voice.

The child struggled valiantly with her emotions, but then fell sobbing into Cecilia's arms. "I'm sowwy, Mommy. I'm sowwy."

"I know you are," she said, dropping to her knees and cradling the little girl in her arms. "I know you are." Tears clogged her throat and burned her eyes as she lifted her daughter and carried her to the rocker in the corner.

Anne-Elizabeth's wracking sobs abated slowly as the chair's steady motion calmed her, until even her childish whimpers silenced and her breathing became even. Her red hair pressed damply to her forehead, she appeared almost angelic in Cecilia's arms, incapable of the rage and confusion and hurt that had driven her to such an act.

"It's not fair," Cecilia whispered softly, her eyes meeting Jeff's in silent entreaty.

A few minutes later she carried Anne-Elizabeth upstairs and laid her gently on her eyelet-covered bed, then tucked her favorite purple blanket around her. When Cecilia straightened, she saw Jeff standing in the doorway.

"You've gotta admit we were pretty lucky," Jeff whispered as they retraced their steps down the stairs.

"How?" she asked, pausing.

"If she bit Monica just for kissing Robert, can you imagine what she would have done if she'd seen us?"

A giggle bubbled up from her throat. "How could you bring that up at a time like this?" she demanded, popping him on the shoulder with her clenched fist. "You're just as obnoxious as you always were."

"Not really," he disagreed. He pulled her close and wrapped an arm around her as they descended the remaining stairs.

"What next?" she asked, sitting down on the bottom step.

"Around this house? There ain't much telling, kid." He dropped down beside her, casting a cautious glance around. "What happened to the others?"

Cecilia shrugged wearily. "They're out playing, I guess."

Jeff took one of her hands in his, his thumb rubbing gentle circles in her palm. "I guess I ought to go." His tone was wistful.

Cecilia longed to sink against him, to draw from his strength. But this time the strength had to be hers.

Jeff raised her hand to his lips and pressed a gentle kiss on her fingers. "All right, kid, I'm leaving." He smiled sadly, sensing her reluctance. "When can I see you again?"

"I've got a heavy schedule next week," she hedged.

"You always have a heavy schedule," he repeated, his dark brows lowered in concern. "Seems to me you ought to be able to get away from your responsibilities at least occasionally."

She just shook her head. "It's not as easy as that."

"I'll call you." He bent over and brushed his lips against her temple. "Don't get up. I'll let myself out."

Cecilia remained still, buffeted by conflicting emotions, until he was gone.

The clattering of footsteps gave her advance warning of Brad's and Peter's approach. Brad squeezed in beside her on the stairs, and Peter sat at her feet.

"I think Jeff's nice, Mom. Don't you?" Brad asked, his face turned expectantly up to hers.

"I still say he's a jerk." Peter's tone was adamant.

Cecilia looked from one son to the other.

Oh, boy.

Cecilia spread the photographs in front of her on the breakfast bar. After two games the number was increasing steadily. There were several of Peter, one of which was quite good. He had leaped into the air to head the ball, and Jeff had caught him precisely at the moment of contact—ball sailing, hair flying, feet inches above the ground and arms outthrust as if he were attempting to fly.

Both photos of Anne-Elizabeth captured her playing in the dirt on the sidelines, totally oblivious to the action behind her on the field.

But the stack of pictures with Brad in them was thick. One caught him arguing a call with a referee. His red hair was mussed and damp with perspiration, and his chin jutted forward pugnaciously as he waved his hands in the air to make a point. Cecilia had been appalled, and had threatened to pull him off the field if he ever behaved that way again. But the photograph so aptly captured the eight-year-old's spirit, she knew it would always hold a special place in her album.

She also knew she was having a difficult time keeping the photographer from stealing a special place in her heart. *Damn you, Jefferson Smith. You show up when I desperately need a friend, and try to be more. Then when I think I might be ready for more, you start acting like a friend.*

She glanced at the calendar on the wall beside her. The last week of March. And this weekend Robert had custody of the kids. Robert and Monica would take them to their games on Saturday, and Robert had dropped a few hints about a special treat on Sunday.

She sipped her coffee and stared at the photos. A whole weekend without them. Once that thought would have seemed like heaven. Today it was frightening. Would Anne-Elizabeth behave herself? Would Brad and Peter fight and get on Monica's nerves?

The phone jangling at her elbow startled her.

"Lookin' good, babe."

"How can you tell, Mitch?"

"You haven't forgotten rehearsal tonight, have you?"

"Mitch, I went over all this with your uncle. We aren't doing anything new, and I really don't have time—"

"Well, it's like this, Cecilia. Since Uncle Stan left me in charge, I decided to do a few new numbers. Some fun stuff, for April Fools', you know?"

Cecilia felt a jab of apprehension. "What are you trying to pull, Mitchell Delaney?"

"Pull? Me?" Even over the telephone, his voice lacked the innocence he was striving for.

"And besides…I really don't want to sing that night. I'm not sure that I'll be available," she hedged.

"Cecilia, you can't leave me high and dry at this late date! How would I ever replace you? Besides, nobody else has your versatility, and that's paramount at this point."

"I'm sure you'd manage." But even as she said the words, she felt a sinking feeling in her stomach. Who was she trying to kid? She needed the money too badly to pass up the opportunity. And what was one more rehearsal, one more night? "Okay, what time are we on for tonight?"

"We won't need you till 9:30. Does that give you enough time to take care of your kids?"

"Sure. I'll be there." She hung up. If it wasn't one thing, it was another. Stan was always content to do the same material, over and over again. If anything, he was a little too stuck in his rut. But Mitch . . . no telling what songs he had in mind.

Well, two could play at that game. There was a particular song that had been driving her crazy lately. . . .

She headed for the stereo and flipped through her albums until she had three in her hand. Which rendition did she want to hear—Garland, Streisand or Ronstadt?

Sitting cross-legged in front of the stereo, she closed her eyes and let the music wash over her. " 'I'm wild again, beguiled again . . . a quivering, shivering child again. . . .' "

The telephone rang three times before she forced herself to cut off the music and answer. Impatient at the interruption, she responded with a breathless "Hello."

"Well, I've received more enthusiastic greetings in my day."

"Jeff," she said, immediately straightening on the bar stool. "Hi, what's up?"

"That's what I wanted to ask you, kid. Do you think you could get away for dinner tonight? I have a client to entertain, and he's bringing his wife. I thought maybe you'd enjoy some time out from the heathens."

Her mood settled even deeper into the doldrums. "Sorry, I can't. I have a rehearsal."

"Well, it was worth a try. Maybe I could drop by afterward."

Mitchell Delaney, I could strangle you! She dug her nails into a coffee-stained dish towel and choked back a "yes," settling instead for a dispirited "I wish you could, too, but there's absolutely no way. I'll be out until the wee hours."

"Maybe next time." He sounded as disappointed as she was. "How often do you have to do this—stay out so late on a week night? What do you do about the kids?"

"It happens pretty often, I suppose, though Stan lets me skip out on rehearsals as often as he can. I have a high school girl who comes in when I need her."

Jeff's chuckle sent a warm current bubbling through her veins. Lord, what she wouldn't do to be able to spend a few hours, a few minutes even, with him. But she closed her eyes and conjured up an image of the money she'd be making from Mitch's gig.

"I'm flying down to Houston for three days around the first of the month. I guess that's next week, isn't it?"

Her spirits plummeted further, and she rubbed her throbbing temples. Just as well she hadn't backed out of the convention.

"Cecil...." His voice dropped a few decibels. "I wish there were some way I could do this in person, but I can't so... consider yourself kissed."

"Ditto," she replied. And then, on a gentle sigh, she added, "Thanks. I needed that."

Cecilia entered the church basement where Stan's band practiced, and blinked in surprise. The usual group had swelled to almost twice its dozen members, and from the youth and wild appearance of the extra musicians, it appeared Mitch had drafted some of his friends from the university.

"Hey, babe, lookin' good," he greeted her, showing her to the stool and mike in front of the band. "Perfect timing. We're ready for you. Hope you're a quick study."

He shoved a notebook filled with sheet music at her and turned back to the band. "Okay, from the top."

The blaring brass introduction, along with a grinding rhythm suggestive of speakeasies and burlesque, almost knocked her off the stool. "What in the world?" she asked, but Mitch didn't hear her over the music. She opened the folder to find the vocals for "Minnie the Moocher" on top.

"Is this some kind of joke?" she demanded. But then a giggle rose from her throat. Stan would absolutely die if he had any idea. When her cue came, she was helplessly in tears, laughing harder than she had in a long time. Somehow she choked out the first few bars, then slid into the mood.

By the time they got to the chorus of "Hidy-hidy-hidy-hoes" her reservations had melted away, and the band members were repeating each line with unleashed enthusiasm. They finished on a blaring high note, then burst into hoots and applause.

"You know," Mitch said regretfully when the tumult had died down, "I really wanted to do 'Just a Gigilo,' but I couldn't figure out how to pull it off with a female singer."

"Thank goodness for small favors," Cecilia retorted, reaching for a tall glass of water. "Mitch, I hate to tell you this, but one more like that and I won't have any vocal chords left."

"Okay. Once through was plenty. And we'll save it for late—the foot doctors'll be more in the mood for it after a few drinks under their belts, anyway."

The podiatrists had no idea what they were in for.

Jeff had originally entered Fiona's Shear Ecstasy establishment with an apprehensive shudder. But after seven years of sharing the same office building and handling all her financial records from her divorces to her taxes to her buy-out of the salon, he had grown accustomed to her particular brand of panache. Pushing through the stained glass doors, he was relieved to see the back of Fiona's blond, corkscrewed head. At least he wouldn't have to risk Trevor and his punk scissors.

"Ready?" Jeff asked.

She nodded and gestured Jeff back to the shampoo room. Minutes later he was just settling into the yellow contoured chair in her bay, when Fiona appeared over his shoulder in the mirror, gleaming scissors in hand. "The usual?"

"The usual."

"Oh, you conservative accountant types are no fun at all. With this hair, I could do magnificent things." She fingered a damp, curly tendril. "It's sinful. Just sinful."

"The usual," Jeff repeated firmly.

Fiona combed and clipped, spritzing with an occasional squirt of water, jabbering nonstop about her love life, her financial woes, her astrological forecast.

"How's your little girl?" Jeff interrupted suddenly.

Fiona stopped in mid-clip, mid-sentence, mid-breath. Her blue eyes widened in mock-shock and her mouth formed a perfect circle of surprise. "Why, Jeff, is this a personal interest you're taking, after all these years?"

Flaming color crept up his neck and flooded his face. "I didn't mean . . . I mean, I didn't mean to say . . ."

Fiona tossed her blond head back and crowed with laughter. "Don't lose your breakfast, sweets. You just caught me off guard. I imagine you remember every detail of my financial affairs, but somehow I never figured you'd remember Brandi." She snipped a little more, then winked. "And she's just fine, thank you. Gorgeous, absolutely beautiful. I'm thinking about placing her with an agency, letting her do some modeling."

It was Jeff's turn for dismay. "How old is she?"

"Four-and-a-half. Five in October. Blond hair, blue eyes . . ." Fiona grinned. "A winning combination if ever there was one."

"Who keeps her while you work?"

Fiona's eyes clouded. "A day-care center, right now. She was staying with a neighbor, but it didn't work out."

"But you're home nights."

"Are you kidding?" She swept a wisp of hair out of her eyes and began snipping the other side of his head. "Since Ramon quit, I've been opening and closing every day except Mondays, and I always work out on Monday nights—exercise to keep the mind healthy, wealthy and strong."

"Hmm." He thought of Cecil, whose turbulent schedule kept her life turned upside down, and how she managed to cope without shortchanging anybody, except maybe herself.

"Well, surely you're going to explain why the sudden interest. Are you thinking of investing in a day-care center or something?"

"Not hardly."

Fiona snatched the drape from his shoulders with a flourish. "*Fini*. And this time I've outdone myself."

Jeff felt a twinge of panic. "What do you mean?"

She pursed her lips in thought. "Yes, I do believe that curly little tail adds just the right touch."

"What?"

She gave the chair a spin and slapped a mirror into his hand as he reached behind and felt his customary smooth neckline.

"April Fools'."

Jeff had written the check and was halfway through the door, when he stopped, spun and said, "April Fools'?"

Fiona cocked her head. "Yes?"

"Damn, how could I have forgotten?" he demanded.

"I'm sure I don't know," she deadpanned back.

"Well, what am I going to do?"

Fiona stroked her cheek with a long, emerald-tipped fingernail, then shrugged. His time was up; her next client was already grabbing the chair.

Ten minutes later, in his office, he had reassigned the Houston trip to McVay.

Jeff considered the departure of one of his most precious accounts with a shudder of apprehension, but not because

McVay couldn't handle it. She could. What bothered him was that turning it over to her was so easy. Canceling the trip to Houston was easy. Wrecking his schedule for the entire weekend was easy.

He wasn't acting like himself at all.

April Fool, indeed.

Seven

Cecilia stepped from the service elevator and wove her way among tall, multitiered serving carts and bustling waiters to reach the grand ballroom where the podiatrists were in the midst of their banquet. Once through the swinging doors, the behind-the-scenes bustle of the hotel staff took a sharp turn to the elegant. A colossal chandelier illuminated the immense room with subdued splendor; the carpet was thick, plush green, patterned with gold fleurs-de-lis. A hundred candlelit tables occupied by conventioneers and their spouses surrounded the parquet dance floor.

"Ooh-la-la!" Mitch's eyes twinkled and he held his arms wide, a baton in one hand, a gleaming silver trumpet in the other, as Cecilia stepped onto the bandstand. "Cecilia, you're wonderful."

"Thank you," Cecilia said primly, fluffing her curls with her red-lacquered nails. The black feather boa she'd snatched from the back of her closet on a whim fluttered with every movement, tickled with the slightest breeze.

Mitch tipped his stout torso toward his trumpet case and produced a tissue-wrapped parcel from within the old-fashioned mute. "For you, my lady."

The distinctive fragrance hit her before she'd uncovered the creamy white petals. "A gardenia. Why, Mitch, how...how quaint." Her lashes fluttered and she laughed to hide the catch in her throat. A flower, tonight of all nights, was fitting. She pinned it high on the shoulder of her contour-fitting, black satin dress, then spun in a half circle, relishing the swirl of the gored satin skirt at mid-calf.

"You look ravishing," he said expansively. "Straight out of the forties." He tapped his baton on the music stand, and gradually the band quieted from its subtle, warming-up sounds to an expectant silence.

Dishes clattered and glasses clinked in the background. Voices murmured and laughter crackled as the podiatrists and their spouses, sated and wined, lingered over their last evening before dispersing to the four corners of the nation.

Cecilia stood at the microphone and adjusted her boa. Contrary to custom, Mitch was foregoing the usual instrumental dance tune intended to lure the more dedicated or attention-seeking dancers onto the floor. Instead she heard his low-voiced, "One, two, one, two, three, four," and four bars of rousing intro. It was up to her. She stepped forward. "'Come on, baby, let the good times roll...'"

Stunned faces angled up at her as the blaring music shattered the serene mood.

"'Come on, baby, let me thrill your soul...'"

Her lids lowered; her fingers snapped; a sultry half smile curved her lips. "'Roll all night long.'"

She felt that familiar electric tingle rippling up her back, down her shoulders, and was only vaguely aware as the dance floor filled. Mitch's plan was working so far. Before the evening was over, she would strut all her "voices," crooning heartbreaking ballads, warbling country/swing and belting out roadhouse blues. And damn, it felt good.

After finishing the first set of vocals, she finally was able to drop to a small padded stool behind the drums and grab a tall glass of ice water from a tray, catching a drip with a linen napkin before it could spatter her skirt. She dabbed her forehead with the cool, damp fabric, relieved to be off her feet and out of the public eye for a few numbers. She slipped her right pump off and rubbed her little toe. She'd forgotten how much these shoes pinched.

And then she noticed the note on the tray. "SONG-BIRD" was scrawled across the paper in bold, black letters. She sighed in disgust as she unfolded the note. "I'd like to meet you. Room 1123 after the dance. Your admirer, Dr. Myron Rhodentucker." Just as she'd anticipated.

Cecilia crushed the paper in her fist. "I must have forgotten and twitched," she grumbled.

"Twitched?" Jeff's voice repeated in her ear.

Stunned, she twisted on the stool and saw him towering over her. Her mouth fell open. "Jeff?"

"Shh..." He raised a finger to his lips, then pointed to the name tag on his lapel that read Hello! My name is Myron Rhodentucker, Peoria, Illinois.

"Where did you get—what are you—"

"Hush." Jeff sat beside her. "I'm operating on the thin assumption that since he didn't pick up his name tag before dinner, Dr. Rhodentucker left the convention early."

"But what if he shows up?" She stifled a giggle. "What if someone sees you and knows you're not...Myron."

"Why do you think I'm hanging around behind the band?"

"Because you're making advances to the singer."

"Sheer coincidence."

"Seriously, Jeff," Cecilia said. "What are you doing here?"

"Being with you."

She gulped and glanced away, and caught Mitch staring curiously at them. "You're ruining my reputation."

"How do I continue to do that without actually getting any of the side benefits?" The corner of his mouth quirked up. "Ruining a good woman's reputation should be more lascivious, more titillating, more scandalous, don't you think?"

"In this kind of job I have to bend over backward to keep men from thinking I'm open season. I have three ground rules—no alcohol, no men, no exceptions."

"And I, of course, am intoxicating, male, and the exception." He grinned.

"No," she retorted. "And you still haven't answered me. Why did you crash this convention?"

He reached for the boa and twirled one fine feather around his finger. "You look . . . different from yourself tonight."

"Not different from myself. Just different from the way you usually see me." She was mesmerized by his nearness, by the way his hand came so close to touching her bare arm, but didn't. The music shifted into a Cole Porter standard, the last number before her next vocal. Mitch had stopped staring, but Cecilia didn't feel any less exposed.

Her throat was dry. "I thought you were flying to Houston."

"I sent McVay, instead."

"Why, Jeff?"

He continued to play with the feathers, brushing them this way and that without ever quite touching her skin, yet she tingled with the awareness of it. "I couldn't bear the thought of you spending your birthday alone."

"My birth—" She felt a flush spreading across her cheeks. "How did you know?"

"April Fools'?" His hand fell away from her, and his smile was gentle, teasing. "How could I forget?"

Cecilia's fingers fondled the velvety gardenia petals on her shoulder. "I don't know what to say."

"How about, 'Yes, I'll meet you in room 1123 after the dance'?"

"*What?*" Her fist clenched and the poor gardenia caught the worst of it.

"That was a joke. But really, Cecil, do you mind?"

When she didn't respond immediately, he repeated, "Do you mind if I stay? I don't want to create problems for you."

He was creating problems right and left. But still, she found herself saying, "I don't mind."

"Then maybe . . . afterward, we could have dinner."

After a night's work she'd be exhausted, and definitely not hungry. But, what the heck? It was her birthday. And he was Jeff.

And she refused to examine the significance of the latter when she responded, "I'd love to."

* * *

Juggling bags, Jeff swung open the door of his town house, and Cecilia stepped into the cool, sophisticated simplicity that greeted her. She walked across the polished marble floor of the small foyer and thought of the muddy footprints she hadn't had time to wipe from the floor at home. Night and day.

When she reached the Oriental rug in the living room, a squawking, screeching, vocal assault sent her flying into Jeff's arms. "Good grief—what is it?"

"Give 'em hell, Harry!"

"It's only Toulouse," he explained, laughing. But he held her securely. "My uncle's parrot."

"Give 'em hell, Harry!" the bird screeched again.

"Is he going to attack?"

"Come on. He can't hurt you." Jeff touched a switch and the living room was flooded with light. But before she could register the effect of the startlingly vivid painting on the opposite wall, the squawking, which had stopped momentarily, reached a new frenzy.

"Hey, buddy," Jeff said in a soothing tone of voice and snatched a handful of sunflower seeds from an Oriental jar.

But the bird refused to be distracted, and Cecilia was obviously the target of his wild-eyed wing-beating fury.

It didn't matter that the feathered beast was in a cage bigger than she was. She backpedaled toward the door, her eyes frozen on the gaping, hooked beak.

"I really don't know what's gotten into him," Jeff said. "He's probably just mad because I didn't come home earlier for dinner."

Cecilia stared at the orange eyes. The orange eyes glared back. "I don't think that's his problem." She shuddered. "He hates me."

"Don't be ridiculous. He's a bird. He's incapable of hating you." But the uncertain glance Jeff aimed in her direction when Toulouse shrieked maniacally belied his words. "I'll give him some mango and let him out on his perch. That'll calm him down."

"You let that bird out of that cage and I'll—I'll—" The threat died on her lips when Jeff left the room. She exchanged venomous glares with the bird.

"Hussy."

Cecilia's mouth fell open.

"Brazen hussy!"

"Jeff, your uncle's bird is insulting me!"

The bird screeched, then cocked its head and glowered. "Round up the usual suspects."

"What?" Appalled, she called out to Jeff, "What is this crazy bird talking about?"

The parrot fanned the green feathers on its neck. Its eyes were glowing orange accusations at her. "If she can stand it, I can. Play it!"

Jeff returned with a palmful of mango pieces. "He's usually not so distraught. This isn't like him at all."

"So you keep telling me," Cecilia muttered from her spot safely in reach of the French doors on the other side of the room.

Jeff deposited the fruit in the cage. "There you go, you crotchety old bag of feathers."

"When is your uncle taking him back?"

"Never. He died three years ago. Left Toulouse to me in his will."

"Oh. I'm sorry." For the first time, Cecilia noticed the seed shells and feathers spattering the otherwise immaculate carpet, and knew instinctively how much of an adjustment Jeff had had to make. "What a dreadful inheritance. Do you ever consider giving him away?"

Jeff sighed, wiping his hands on his handkerchief. "When Uncle Harry asked me to take care of Toulouse, I didn't realize how much trouble a bird could be." His laugh was wry. "I can't imagine anyone else putting up with him for long."

"I can't imagine you putting up with him at all." Cecilia's gaze swept the room. "Especially you."

"Brazen hussy!" Toulouse squawked.

"You know, he doesn't like females in general."

"I can't tell you how relieved I am," Cecilia said, straight-faced. "What are you, a student of bird psychology, or something?"

"When I inherited him I read a lot about Amazon parrots." Jeff opened the door of a teakwood cabinet. At least a dozen books on parrots, particularly double yellow heads, were neatly arranged. "I read somewhere that when this type of parrot is raised exclusively by one person, they can get rather hostile toward other people, especially those of the opposite sex. Uncle Harry lived alone, so..."

"Give 'em hell!"

"Rather hostile." Cecilia sniffed.

"Why don't we leave him alone until he calms down?"

"Why don't we just leave him alone indefinitely."

"Why, Cecil, I believe you're afraid of that bag of feathers." Jeff was clearly amused.

"He has a beak that would puncture an armored tank and talons like razors, all of which he'd like to sink into me. Why should I be afraid?"

Jeff led her into a dining area and sat her down in front of the table where he'd spread a selection of take-out Chinese food.

"Open your mouth and eat," Jeff ordered sternly, then softened it with a grin. He popped open two cans of soda and slid one across the table to her.

At this late hour they were both too hungry to chat at first. After finishing off her fried rice, Cecilia paused, a shrimp dripping sweet-and-sour sauce halfway to her mouth. "No candles, no seductive music, no strong drink. What kind of bachelor are you?"

"The kind who's trying very hard not to scare you off."

A piece of shrimp lodged in her throat. She choked and sputtered, "Oh, my."

"I'd rather not scare myself off, either, if you'd like to know the truth," he admitted over the top of his soda can. "So, tonight, let's just be old friends."

"Oh. Old friends." She sipped from her pop. "That's fair enough." So why did the flutterings in her stomach suddenly quiet into a disappointed lump? She slid a glance around the room. "I would like some music, though."

"I should think you'd be tired of it."

"Tired of Mitch Delaney's shenanigans, yes. Tired of music? Never."

"I am totally amazed at the way you sing."

Cecilia chewed her food deliberately.

"How do you do it? All those songs were so different—and so were you, for each one."

"You've heard of being multilingual? Well, I'm multi-singual. You name it, I do it. I twang, I grate, I croon, I swoon, I can choke back a sob or grind out a threat, all in perfect pitch." She smiled, quite unabashed at her own boastfulness. "It's what makes me such a valuable commodity."

"Valuable?"

"Sure. A commercial singer has to be versatile above all."

"And a damn good singer."

She shrugged. "That goes without saying. But my point is, there are a lot of damn good singers out there who couldn't last an hour in a commercial jingle studio because they lack the adaptability. I just happen to be someone who can."

"And it's steady?"

"Getting steadier all the time." Cecilia toyed with a barbecued rib. "The elite in our business make upward of a hundred grand a year."

"Good grief!" Jeff almost sputtered his cola, but managed to get control of himself. "And you . . . you're in that category?"

She shook her head. "Nope. Not yet. But I plan to get there."

"That should take care of your bouncing checks?" he teased, eyes dancing.

"Jeff, my checks didn't bounce because I overspent. I'm just a haphazard bookkeeper. And my checking account runs low because I keep stashing money in savings for my education."

Jeff set down his glass thoughtfully "You know, for someone who's planning a career in education, you certainly have a talent for postponing it. You haven't taken a single class in . . . how many years?"

"I'm going to," she began defensively. Hadn't she been through the same hassle with Robert? "I've just been too busy."

"And profitably so, it would seem."

"Well . . . yes," she admitted, mollified.

"Cecilia, tell me the truth. Do you even went to be a music teacher?"

"I love kids. I would be very good at it."

"That's not what I asked."

Damn him. She met his gaze head-on, and was furious at him for asking the single question nobody else had asked. "It's not exactly what I want, but I love music, and I think I'd be very happy teaching. Plus it's so practical. I'd work the same hours and have the same holidays as the kids, and—"

"Cecilia Evans, I'm ashamed of you."

"For what?" she asked.

"For deluding yourself so totally." Jeff shook his head in wonderment. "Since when has practicality been your motive for anything?"

"But it makes so much more sense than—"

"Than continuing in a career that could prove so financially rewarding?" He reached across the table and covered her hand with his, and she couldn't move, could only stare at him. "And even more important, a career that you love?"

"I—I don't know."

"I think you've been listening to the wrong advice, Cecil."

She closed her eyes, wondering if he realized how close he'd called it. Robert was the one hounding her to get on with her plans, to go back to school, to be realistic, to be practical. She felt a tremor of distaste and rebellion. Was she still under Robert's influence—he who always knew what was best for everybody—without realizing it?

She jerked her hand away and laughed nervously. "How did we get on this subject? Oh, I remember," she rushed on. "I was asking for music."

"The stereo system's in the living room. I suppose we could—"

Her eyes widened at the thought of his ill-natured parrot. "Never mind. Forget it."

"There is another option."

Cecilia put down her glass. "Such as?"

He seemed to reconsider, then finally pushed away from the table. "Come with me."

She skipped to keep up with his long-legged stride as he dragged her across the entryway, up the narrow stairs, toward a closed doorway. He opened the door and flipped on the light. "Excuse the mess," he said. "I never use this room, so it just catches things."

Cecilia glanced around. What mess? A few cartons stacked neatly, yes. Odds and ends of furniture arranged systematically, yes. And oddly out of place, a battered old upright piano, its warm oak veneer cracked with age.

Jeff pulled the old-fashioned stool out and took his place on it. "*Voilà*. Music."

"I just sing. I don't play."

"But I do." Jeff rippled a twangy, off-key scale from bottom to top. He winced. "I didn't realize it needed tuning so badly."

"I had no idea you played the piano," she said, sitting on the corner of a cracked leather ottoman.

"By the time I was in high school, I'd managed to bury that character flaw in my deep, dark past."

"Character flaw?" she demanded.

"I hated every minute I ever spent playing the piano." He ran another scale up the keyboard.

"This piano?" she asked.

"No. This was Uncle Harry's. He loved music."

"Too bad he didn't love canaries," she muttered. "You've kept his bird, which is disgusting, and his piano, which you hate. You must have loved him very much."

Jeff seemed to concentrate on his hands as they slowed. "Uncle Harry wasn't very lovable—at least, I didn't think so when I was a kid. But as I got older, and at the end when he was so sick..." He shrugged. "I think he was just lonely and didn't know how to let people know he cared." He grew still for a moment, then continued, "So I keep Toulouse and the piano to remind me of the kind of man I don't want to be." He swiveled on the squeaky stool and faced her, his eyes shadowed, haunted.

She wanted to touch the corners of his eyes, make them crinkle the way they did when he smiled, to wipe away the emptiness. "I think that's very sad."

He stared at his hands. "That he died a lonely old man?"

"No." She stood, forcing lightness into her tone. "That you spent so many hours hating music. If I had known all this in high school, I would have washed my hands of you."

"You mean, I could have gotten rid of you that easily?"

"Absolutely." She spun him back to face the piano. "What do you remember?"

"I don't know." He ran his fingers over the keyboard, then began a Bach fugue. "How's this?"

"Fine, if you're dead. Let's see . . ." She eyed the piano, a dilapidated collection of warped wood, rusty strings and chipped keys, and inspiration struck. "Do you know, 'Bad, Bad Leroy Brown'?"

Jeff shook his head. "But how about . . ." His fingers flew, and suddenly the piano seemed capable of making music. Even the occasional twang sounded appropriate as he played the beginning of "Alexander's Ragtime Band."

"That's it! That's it! Wait a minute!" Cecilia dragged the ottoman to the corner of the piano and hopped on, then, with no thought to propriety or grace, boosted herself up and climbed atop the upright. "I'd better not get splinters," she said, giggling.

"Don't worry, I'd pick them out for you," he replied suggestively.

"'Come on and play, Come on and play, Alexander's Ragtime Band.'" Her voice was husky from too much singing already, but the music seemed to spring from her as she dangled the boa and tickled Jeff's nose. "'It's the best band in the land.'"

He shook his head and laughed, filling in the melody with more fullness as he became more sure of himself.

She stretched across the top of the piano and swung the boa as she tapped out the syncopation against the wall with her foot. She tossed her head back and laughed, full throated and jubilant. "Isn't this grand?"

"No, it's an upright," Jeff deadpanned.

"Shoot the piano player," she declared dramatically.

"No, he's doing—"

"The best he can," she said, finishing the quotation with him, then collapsing in a spate of giggles.

"If I didn't know better, I'd think you were drunk."

"No." And to prove it, she sobered immediately. "Just exhausted to the very core of my bones, and..." She held the word back, afraid to release it, lest he attach too much significance to it. But it came all the same. "Happy."

His gaze softened and the music slowed to a long chord. "I feel honored to have made you happy."

"You, the night, even that darned old bird. But especially you." She rolled onto her back, her legs dangling off the edge of the piano, and closed her eyes. "I can feel the music going right through me. I can't explain it. It vibrates through me. Sometimes it happens when I'm not even around music. But this time the music's real—thrumming right into my bones. I love it."

"It's a good thing I don't know Leroy Brown. It would have knocked you right off the top." He changed the tempo and key. "How about this?"

The old song gently worked its way into her, and she felt herself smiling. "Play it again, Sam."

"No. 'Play it. If she can stand it, I can.'"

"That's what the stupid bird said."

"I know. I taught him." He chuckled.

"I believe you actually like that disgusting old bird."

"Well," he said thoughtfully, hitting a sour note and quickly correcting it, "you like Peter, so I guess we're even."

Cecilia slashed the end of the boa at him.

"I'm crushed." He obviously wasn't.

"This is nice," she murmured, relaxing again. "I could lie here all night, I think. It's better than a lullaby." The "all night" had slipped out without thinking, and she didn't bother to retract it. Surely he knew what she meant. Old friends. There was a certain comfort in that, even if a part of her did long for...

A warm hand closed over her swinging wrist. She rolled to face him. Their gazes locked. And still his right hand kept up the slow, sad melody. *A kiss is just a kiss, a sigh is just a sigh...*

"Your fingers smell good," he murmured, his thumb against her wrist, charting the erratic pulse.

"That's because they squeezed a gardenia," she forced herself to explain. But he didn't let go. Slowly, almost hesitantly, he pressed her palm against his cheek, watching her. She fought for her voice. "This would really be a mistake."

"I agree." He buried his face in her palm. His breath fanned her skin, warm and moist. "A really big mistake."

The music had stopped, but still she vibrated with it.

"I'm sorry..." she whispered.

He inhaled slowly, then released her hand. "Don't be. We both know this is best."

"No, I mean, I'm sorry that you hated music for all those years. That's the saddest thing I've ever heard."

"Not music. Just piano lessons. But my mother always told me the day would come when I'd be glad. She was right."

"If I'd gotten hold of you sooner..."

He smoothed a strand of hair out of her eyes, brushed a wisp of feather from her cheek. "I'd have been your accompanist."

"What a nice idea." Cecilia sat up and bent toward him, the smile on her face almost steady. "My own personal accompanist at my beck and call."

"Cecilia," he said. "Just once... kiss me."

"We've already kissed." She clamped her hands around her waist. "Twice."

"You're keeping count?"

She flushed.

"So am I. Now pay the accompanist. I promise you, it won't go any farther." His request was so tempting. She found herself remembering not that kissing him would be more dangerous than dancing on thin ice, but that his lips were so soft, so teasing, so delicious.... "Old friends," she murmured, hoping to shake a little sense into him, since she was so sadly in lack of it. "Remember?"

"Old friends." He stood up, his expression not at all sensible.

She leaned closer, her lips parting even before they touched his. One kiss, no farther, no harm.

At first only their lips met. The melting started, spread slowly, gently through her body, until there wasn't a joint that wouldn't have considered jelly an improvement. Gracious, the man could kiss.

And then, that wasn't enough. She reached for him, twining her fingers into his hair, pulling him closer. Only one kiss, but this time she was going to make it last, make it go on forever. There was no harm in that. A forever kiss...one that couldn't be forgotten, even after it ended. She stroked his lips with her tongue, felt them part, then felt his arms wrapping her in possessive strength as she explored the inner contours of his mouth, searching, charting for future memories....

He groaned, one hand reaching up to catch the back of her head and pull her closer. She felt herself being lifted and fell into his arms, felt them both sinking, until the piano stool creaked beneath their weight, and still she didn't break the contact that would end their precious kiss. Just one, he had promised. Nothing more.

His hair was warm silk beneath her hands, thick and glossy, holding the warmth just for her pleasure. His ear, smooth and perfectly shaped, gave her tantalizing new territory to map with her fingertips. She must have tickled him, for he shuddered, and she dragged her hand across the roughness of his jaw, her thumb finding the corners of their mouths and tracing the feel of a perfect kiss...again, to remember. Always to remember...no harm in remembering.

And then, like everything, it ended, not with a bang, but with a whimper that she couldn't stop from escaping her lips. "Old friends," he groaned.

"Very old," she murmured, resting her cheek against his neck.

And then his mouth had captured hers again, silencing, demanding, almost punishing. She gave herself up to his kiss, letting the intensity of his feelings sweep her away. She could do that, she knew. Because beneath their ill-suppressed passion was the constant assurance that neither of them was willing to let their relationship go farther....

His hand slid beneath the satin skirt, covered her thigh, stroked and teased and skimmed the silky surface until the nylons ended. His hand stopped, explored the garter snap, then found the band of exposed skin.

And still she didn't panic. In fact, she felt ripples of pleasure as his lips skimmed down her neck and then kissed it at its base. She tilted her head back, giving him more neck to tantalize. "Jeff, I was just thinking," she whispered. "We were never friends."

"What?" His gaze burned into her, not believing, afraid to believe, what she might be, shouldn't be, yet definitely was, saying.

"You despised me," she reminded him. "I adored you. But we were never, ever, friends."

"Cecil, you have a point."

A garter snap popped free, then another.

Eight

———

Jeff lifted her, and her world rocked gently. His lips found hers again, robbing her of reason, of thought. He tore himself away from her and grated, "You've tangled us in your boa."

And somehow she had. It curled around them, binding them together with wispy strength. Slowly, carefully, she began unwinding it. When her upper arm brushed his face, she felt his lips capture the soft flesh for a bare moment, and shivers skimmed over her. She dragged the boa free of his neck, and the way he closed his eyes and clenched his jaws and tensed made her do it again. Finally the boa was a snaky black coil at their feet. She felt herself easing down his body until she, too, was standing.

A big mistake.

They both knew it, and neither one was doing anything about it. She reached behind herself, but his hands were there first, dragging the zipper down, notch by slow notch. And then, before she could even slide the dress from her shoulders, she felt her bra released, and ignored the alarm jangling in her head. One time . . . to last forever.

The satin dress, so carefully planned to be becoming yet nonrevealing, suddenly was gone, and revealed everything. She then caught his head and pulled it to her. "Please," she whispered, guiding his lips to her breasts, arching in agonized pleasure when he captured their fullness in his hands, lifted them to taste, first with flicking touches of his lips, then with a deep, tugging suction as he worked first one, then the other to a glistening peak.

His lips traveled down, his hands smoothing the wispy garter belt over the soft curve of her stomach, down her legs, and then they, too, were bare, exposed, lightly tanned with the faded sprinkle of freckles.

"Do you have them everywhere?" he asked lightly, though the finger that traced across her thigh hinted that his question was loaded.

"Just about," she said, her voice tinged with disgust.

"You must be very sweet," he murmured.

She shook her head, confused, as his finger dragged dangerously near the juncture of her thighs. She caught her lower lip with her teeth.

"Freckles," he said, "are angel kisses. Sweet angel kisses." He lowered his head to her thigh and began nibbling a trail, from "kiss" to "kiss" to "kiss"....

"I don't have any there," she gasped.

She would have fallen had his hands not cupped her and held her erect. She grabbed his shoulders to push him away but couldn't, only stood there, quaking under the expert assault of his breath, his lips, his tongue.... She couldn't breathe, she couldn't move, she couldn't... And then, a low keening cry tearing from her in soft gasps, the tremors rippled through her, radiating in ever widening circles of shuddering pleasure, until she was nothing but a pool of quivering sensation, helpless to his will.

Stop, she wanted to say, but she didn't want him to, didn't want to admit it, couldn't. Then, when she was certain she'd tear apart if he didn't stop, she was sinking, dropping, then pressed against his chest, her heart thundering with his as his hands explored, soothed, spread warm comfort, took away the shock, the embarrassment.

"Oh, my," she whimpered softly. "I've never... I didn't know it would—" And then, lest he misunderstand she hurriedly added, "Of course I have, but never that way!" She caught her breath again as he brushed her breast with one palm, watched her nipple harden, whispered his palm across its tip again, watching it rise and fall with her quickening breath. "Oh, my," she said, sighing again, reaching to unbutton his shirt.

He tore it off, popping a button in the process, and jerked his belt free with one hand. She found herself watching, devouring him with her eyes, realizing that none of her adolescent fantasies had prepared her for the reality of Jefferson Smith. Adolescent fantasies... She felt herself flush with embarrassment, and turned her head as he began removing his trousers. In all her life, she'd seen only one man naked, and he had been her husband. She was a grown woman, yet she felt naive. Jeff's legs were long and dusted with silky dark hairs, his chest furred with it.

This was no fantasy, and she was no shy young miss, asking for more than she was willing to give. She wasn't afraid; she wasn't ashamed; she was simply...aware. Aware of a boundary crossed, and as his hands touched her again, she shivered with longing and acceptance. She wanted it all, everything he had to give her.

He carried her into the dark bedroom, his arms tightening around her as he lowered her to his bed, the thin shaft of light from the hallway touching their bodies with golden light amidst the shadows. She liked the darkness and the freedom it gave her to touch and explore, to slide her hands over his chest and feel his muscles tense as she explored lower and found the hard, rampant heat of him and felt him shudder at her touch. The magic night seemed to surround them, to pulse between them, hungry and urgent, feeding off their longings, and then he was stretching over her, his hard body pressed against the length of hers, his kisses devouring her neck, her breasts, stoking her with the flames of his desperation.

When his lips finally closed over hers there was no finesse, no gentleness, but a raging desire burning out of control, unrestrained need, a desperate binding of lips and

tongues. She burned with a wildfire that had had its gentle
kindling years before, but now raged beyond the limits of
reason.

"Now," she whispered, and gasped at the exquisite pressure as he settled between her thighs, prolonging the agony
for an excruciating moment.

She arched against him, felt him enter and fill her, their
joining one of a sensual fulfillment as he stroked, first
slowly, then faster, then slowly again, on and on, until she
felt herself shattering again and again, clutching his body
with hers, arching against him, into him, loving him, heaven
help her, loving him, taking whatever he gave her and more,
until he, too, was spent. She spiraled slowly back into the
waiting arms of reality, the strong arms of the man she
loved. Their movements slowed until they lay together in a
gentle rest.

She caressed the lean planes of his face while her lips
murmured lovingly against his own, until he finally rolled
to her side, his hand lingering on her stomach. Cecilia stared
at the ceiling, and felt her silky sensations subside and vague
feelings of unease surface. She toyed with a corner of the
sheet. The silence stretched between them, until finally she
blurted, "What comes next?"

"What?" Jeff stirred beside her, his fingers flexing across
her stomach, then relaxing again.

"I've never done this before."

"You've never done what before? I mean—Cecil, what
are you talking about?" He raised up on his elbow, his
expression one of disbelief and astonishment.

She felt a flush creeping across her body. "I've never
made love with anyone who wasn't my husband. I mean,
I'm lying here in a strange bed, staring at a strange ceiling—"

"If you call me a strange man, I'm throwing you out of
this bed," he threatened.

"No, I wouldn't say that, but—well, you are—"

"A man who isn't your husband. I got that part. Go on."

She couldn't tell if the strain in his voice was from irritation or suppressed amusement. "I don't even know the color
of the walls. Not that it makes any difference, mind you, but

it just makes me feel so strange. I don't want you to get the wrong idea about me." She shifted, dislodging his hand, rolling to face him. "This isn't the kind of thing I usually do. Even for old times' sake. Especially not for old times' sake. You believe that, don't you?"

"Cecil?"

"Yes?"

"You're babbling. You babble when you're nervous."

"I know." She sighed.

"Don't be nervous. Don't explain. I never for one moment thought that you were . . . easy. In fact, I rather hope that what just happened between us was special."

"Oh, it was," she said, more vehemently than she'd intended. His dark silhouette bent toward her. His lips brushed blindly across her cheek, feeling their way to her mouth. It was so much easier just to relax, she decided, and stop worrying about everything. When he kissed her, it felt as if the whole world settled back into place. And when he finally ended the kiss he curled around her, drawing her closer until their bodies were nestled together like spoons.

"Beige."

"What?"

"Beige. The walls are beige."

"Oh. Well, I said it really didn't matter—".

"Sleep."

"Huh? You've totally lost me, Jeff."

"Sleep comes next." His arm curled protectively around her, but his voice was hesitant. "I'd really like you to stay."

"I must be getting decadent in my old age, because . . . I'd like to." Then quietly she added, "I hope this hasn't ruined our friendship."

He slowly stroked her stomach. "You really hadn't ever . . ." He hesitantly let the half-finished question dangle.

"Never."

She felt his chest move against her back, a slow, heavy breathing. Then he confessed, "Neither had I."

"Really?" She didn't know whether to be embarrassed or pleased.

"Really."

"Well..." She sighed, then smiled suddenly. Her laughter came in a spurt, cleansing giggles of relieved tension. "Old friends, my foot." She sank against him and sighed again.

This time it was his laughter that rocked the bed and, after a time, his heartbeat that echoed in her sleep.

A diffused shaft of sunlight teased her eyelids open. She tensed herself to stretch, and her sleep-befuddled mind couldn't fathom the obstruction in the path of where her arms and legs wanted to go. Cautiously she arched her back, and felt strong arms tighten around her. Her heart pounded out of control when she saw the dark swirl of hair on the arm draped around her middle. Dear heaven, how could she feel so warm, so secure, so totally and completely natural in this man's arms? If she was beyond understanding, she also was beyond caring. It was too late to do anything but let the chips fall where they would.

She lifted his arm carefully and began to slide from under the covers. Mission accomplished, she told herself when he rolled back over to his side of the bed. He frowned and mumbled, pulling his pillow to his chest and settling back into sleep. Thank goodness. She needed some time to think.

She padded into the spare room. Ignoring her rumpled dress, she slipped on his shirt. Luckily the missing button wasn't in too disastrous a location, unless one was particularly sensitive about exposing one's navel, which seemed to be a minor point, all things considered.

After a visit to the bathroom downstairs, she wandered into the kitchen, its white ceramic tile countertops gleaming in the morning sunlight. The stainless steel cooktop looked as if it had never felt the heat of a fire or suffered the indignity of a grease spatter. The floor shone cleaner than her glassware and she guessed he must have a maid. She couldn't picture him waxing and mopping.

"Where's the food?" she muttered, surveying the near empty shelves of the refrigerator.

"That *is* food," Jeff said from the doorway.

Cecilia jumped at the sound of his voice. His hands were braced against the top of the doorjamb as he stretched.

Wearing only a pair of faded jeans, his body narrowed from wide shoulders to narrow hips. A thin line of dark hair tapered from his flat stomach and disappeared beneath the waistband of his jeans. Cecilia quickly turned back to the refrigerator, letting the cold air cool her flaming cheeks. She had no business being embarrassed at the sight of a bare chest after all that had transpired the night before.... Her cheeks burned a few degrees higher. It wasn't the sight that startled her; it was her reaction to it.

She cleared her throat. "I certainly don't call grape jelly, green olives, cocktail onions and picante sauce a smorgasbord."

Jeff finished his yawn before explaining patiently, "But if you put the grape jelly with the peanut butter in the cabinet—"

"You'll get a meal my kids would love." She closed the refrigerator door.

"But not you?" He seemed distressed. "I—I wasn't planning breakfast for two, you know."

"Peanut butter on toast is my favorite breakfast," she lied.

"I didn't realize the bread was so old," he said sheepishly. She drew closer and saw the green mold through the plastic. Jeff dropped the bag into the trash can and shrugged.

"Well, here's a banana," she offered, trying to be a good sport.

"Sorry. That's for Toulouse. How about doughnuts?"

Cecilia wrapped her arms around her middle, the cool silk of Jeff's shirt a luxurious sensation compared to her oversize T-shirt nighties. "With raspberry jelly?"

"That can be arranged."

"Sounds wonderful." She started to move around him. "Let me get dressed and—"

"No, I'll go get them while you relax." He snaked his arm around her waist and pulled her back against him. "I get the feeling that rest is something you don't get near enough of."

Cecilia felt the tension ebb from her body as she leaned against him, a smile teasing the corners of her lips. He felt

warm and solid behind her, his chin resting atop her head.
"And you?"

"This time of year, too damned little. Fourteen hour
days, sometimes sixteen, weekends—until the fifteenth of
April."

Cecilia stiffened guiltily. "You need to be working don't
you? I should leave."

"God, no." The stricken expression on his face did more
to reassure her than all the protestations in the world. "I
want you here."

Cecilia folded her arms over his. "I'm glad."

He planted a kiss on her temple. "But we'd better make
the best of today, because for the next two weeks I'll be up
to my ears in W2s."

"Yuk." She twisted in his arms to face him. "Doughnuts?" she reminded him.

"And coffee."

"Fantastic."

A loud squawk sounded from the living room. "Rise and
shine!"

"I'm coming," Jeff called, giving Cecilia's bottom a
good-natured pat. The bird responded with a series of ill-
natured noises. "He's just hungry and wants his cover off,"
he apologized, grabbing the banana. "Want to help feed
him?"

Cecilia managed a tight smile. "You go right ahead. I'll
stay in here. That bird's idea of breakfast is my pinkie finger."

But minutes later Jeff appeared in the doorway again,
Toulouse perched imperiously on his shoulder. "See? Now
that he's fed and—" The bird took one look at Cecilia,
spread his wings and screeched.

"I see." She graciously refrained from a much deserved
"I told you so," as Jeff hustled the bird back into the living
room.

When he reappeared, he had the good grace to appear
abashed. "He's really never behaved this way before."

"Have you got him locked up?"

"No, that's not necessary. He's on his perch by the window, and his wings are clipped so he can't fly."

Cecilia didn't bother to tell him she wouldn't trust that bird not to chew his perch down to the ground, splinter by splinter, to get a chance at her toes.

Jeff flipped the switch on the coffeepot. "I didn't set the timer last night, or it would already be brewed," he apologized. "Now just relax, and I'll be back in a jiffy."

Cecilia plopped into a chair, thinking rebelliously of the massive leather one in the living room, of the stereo system she'd seen, of the record collection she'd love to snoop through.

Damn bird.

The wind was chilly, but it never occurred to Jeff to put the top of the car up. He needed the bracing effects of a cool April morning to clear his head. Doughnuts, for pete's sake. They seemed so boring, so staid. Why hadn't he offered croissants or bagels or . . . anything but boring doughnuts.

He pulled up at a Stop sign beneath a spreading catalpa tree, and other than the low roar of his engine, the morning was silent and clean. A gust sent a spray of the large white catalpa blossoms fluttering into the car. He plucked one off his collar and brushed it against his cheek, then held it under his nose to sniff. Not as sweet as Cecil's gardenia, he thought as he accelerated.

His senses were filled with her. He could smell her, taste her, feel her. There had never been a woman so soft, so warm. Curves. She was all soft curves. Funny how he'd always been drawn to long and slender, legs that went on forever. Cecil's calf was plump where it should be plump, but firm, her ankles slender. Her waist nipped in exactly as it should, but her hips, even her bottom, had the most delightfully feminine contours. . . .

And the sound of her. When she got excited, her voice soared, then dropped, half rasp, half chuckle as she rattled on; in his arms her sighs had been throaty, husky.

Her voice, her face, her hands—they fluttered with excitement, flared with quick anger, softened with exquisite temptation when he least expected it. Did she even know what she was doing to him? And why was he letting it happen?

Why? Because from the moment he'd broken off the Houston trip, he'd felt displaced, not real. He had a merciless workload, yet he couldn't keep his mind on work, and as yet he felt no twinge of guilt. By Monday morning he'd probably be gnashing his teeth in the face of last-minute reality.

But not today. Not while Cecilia waited for him.

He pulled into the small, covered parking spot in front of his town house and cut off the engine. He grabbed the box of doughnuts and bounded up the front steps two at a time. He pushed the front door open and walked into a solid wall of country and western music, with an occasional squawking contribution from Toulouse.

The morning newspaper was scattered across the carpet, the business section tossed to one side, the front page to another. The sports page was spread open and Cecilia lay sprawled on her stomach in front of it, her chin propped on her fists. She raised her head and greeted him with a wide smile. "Incaviglia hit two home runs."

Toulouse glared from his spot high on top of the perch, seemingly enraged by Cecilia's bare, swaying legs, perhaps even contemplating snatching her painted toenails. Jeff, too, found them distracting, but he was certain the nibbles the bird was anticipating were quite different from his own.

"You don't like baseball?" She turned the page.

"Oh, yeah. It's great. I just didn't realize the Rangers' season had started."

She crossed her feet, pointing them ceilingward. "Spring training," she explained, examining the basketball box scores.

"I thought you were afraid of Toulouse."

The bird squawked at the sound of his name, and side-stepped restlessly on the perch.

Cecilia gave the bird a cursory glance. "His perch is brass," she said, as if that were supposed to mean something.

"You're driving him crazy," Jeff remarked.

"Yes. Isn't it grand?" She flashed an evil smile, stuck a tongue out at the parrot, then returned to the newspaper.

"Darn. They're blacking out the Mavericks game, and for what good reason? It's been sold-out for weeks."

"I've got tickets."

"What?" She stared at him, her lips parted in surprise. He wanted to kiss her. "You've got tickets to the Lakers game?"

"If that's who they're playing today. A friend at the office gave them to me, when, er, her plans were changed. She had to leave town unexpectedly." He remembered McVay's expression as she'd pitched them onto his desk. But she was a trooper. She hadn't complained. Only reminded him how much they would have cost from a scalper. "It never occurred to me you'd want to go."

"Jeff, that game starts in three hours. By the time I go home and change clothes and we fight the traffic at Reunion—" She pulled to her feet, and he got a quick flash of navel as his shirtfront flared.

"I guess we'd better hurry," he agreed reluctantly, preceding her into the kitchen. He grabbed the coffeepot and poured each of them a cup, grabbed the creamer and sugar bowl from the shelf.

"Do you have any artificial sweetener?" she asked.

"No. I only use the real thing." What was the point of running all those damned laps if he couldn't eat and drink what he wanted to? "Besides, with the sugar load in that jelly doughnut, I can't imagine an extra teaspoon or two will make that much difference."

"You're right. So, where are the seats?"

"I'll have to look and see." He wasn't about to tell her he hadn't planned to use them. Why the hell had he mentioned those tickets? He didn't want Cecilia in the middle of 17,005 other screaming fans, no matter how terrific the game. He didn't want to share her with them or with anybody. He wanted her here, to turn his apartment upside down with scattered clothes and newspapers. To turn him upside down.

And then it hit him hard. He couldn't have Cecilia without sharing her. These past hours were stolen, for him, for her. They were the rare exception to their everyday routines. Her real life was a horde of children, a dog, a chaotic schedule. Not an oasis from his stress load, but an added dose of it.

He watched her lick a dollop of raspberry jelly from her knuckle, listened to her chatter about the game, and wanted to silence her with a hard punishing kiss. Not because he was angry with her, but because he was angry with himself. Angry for forgetting who and what she was.

Angry for not caring, even now, when he knew how impossible a lasting relationship between them would be. They had always been an impossible combination, hadn't they? That was no surprise.

How much it bothered him, that was the shocker.

He splashed his coffee into the sink. "I think I'd better go get dressed."

"Wear green and blue," she advised him.

He shook his head, unable to hold back a chuckle. "Cecil, I don't have anything even remotely near Mavericks green and blue." And before she could get any other ideas, he added, "And I'm not painting my face."

"All right," she retorted. "Be that way."

As she pranced toward the bathroom, he found it difficult to remember that he was now glad they were spending the afternoon with 17,005 screaming basketball fans.

Cecilia peered warily into the bathroom mirror. She fluffed her curls back into their normal state of confusion and washed her face. Her makeup and false eyelashes from the night before were gone, and she was relieved to meet the eyes of the same Cecilia Evans she always saw. She tugged at the neck of Jeff's shirt, closing it more securely over her cleavage.

The door, already ajar, swung open. Jeff stood there, hair combed, wearing a navy polo shirt and gray chinos.

"Don't you ever knock?" She opened a drawer and located a small tube of toothpaste. "Excuse me," she said, and squeezed the blue gel onto her finger, then rubbed it across her teeth.

"Is that the way you always do it?" Jeff asked.

"When I don't have a toothbrush," she sputtered through the foam.

"Here." He slapped a clear plastic toothbrush down on the counter beside her. "If you're going to do it, do it right."

Cecilia took the toothbrush gratefully, though the thought passed through her mind that the fact that he was in the habit of keeping spare toothbrushes around ought to tell her something. Spitting the last of the foam into the sink and rinsing her mouth out, she glared at him in the mirror.

"You're making me nervous. Why are you staring at me like that?" she demanded.

Jeff grinned. "I'm just waiting for you to get through with my toothbrush."

"*Your*— Oh, gad, I'm going to be sick!" Cecilia stared at the clear plastic in her hand. "You're pulling my leg, aren't you?" she asked hopefully.

"What do you think, that I keep spares for overnight guests?"

"My God, Jeff! How many people have used this thing?"

Jeff's hand closed roughly over hers. "Let's get one thing straight, Cecil. I haven't got a revolving door into my bedroom. I thought you knew me better than that. I'm a monogamist, Cecilia. I don't play around. When I have strong feelings for a woman, she's the only one in my life. And when there's no one special, I don't go in for idle flirtations or one-night stands."

Cecilia steeled against his words. *Don't listen*, she pleaded with herself. *Don't start hoping*. She, too, was a monogamist—so much so that there had never been another man in her life but Robert.

Until last night.

But Jeff had had other women in his life. He'd had other relationships, though none of them had led to marriage. So however faithful Jeff might be, a relationship with him was unlikely to lead anywhere but pain.

He released her wrist, and she forced a smile.

"I think I'd better see what kind of shape my clothes are in."

Cecilia climed the stairs, suddenly deflated. Turning into the spare room, she paused. The dress was wrinkled, of course. The boa was still coiled on the floor. Her wispy underwear lay jumbled with his— *What on earth?*

She pressed her fist against her lips, trying to stifle the sudden spurt of laughter. How had she missed them last night? Well, she hadn't actually been watching. As a matter of fact, she'd deliberately avoided watching.

"Cecil?"

She spun to face him through glittering tears, her mouth still covered, her shoulders shaking.

"What's wrong?" His hands closed over her shoulders.

She shook her head helplessly. She wasn't going to laugh. She couldn't laugh. She refused to.

She exploded with laughter.

Jeff's hands fell away and concern warred with confusion on his face. "What's the problem?"

Cecilia pointed at the red tartan boxer shorts beside her own peacock blue half-slip, then sank to the floor, tears streaming down her face.

Jeff towered over her, his arms akimbo. "Do you have a problem with my shorts?" he demanded.

"They're really yours?" she gasped.

"Who the hell do you think they belong to?"

"They—they don't look like you, Jeff."

"Oh?" he drawled. "And who do they look like?"

"I mean, they just didn't . . . they weren't what . . . Damn it, Jeff!" She glared up at him.

"I don't like people laughing at my shorts," he reprimanded her sternly, and his eyes gleamed with intent. "I'm going to make you pay for that." He grabbed her wrists and applied gentle pressure, pulling her with him to the floor. He pressed her shoulders and she allowed him to pin her to the floor. "Apologize for laughing."

"No. I won't apologize. They looked funny lying on the floor like that." She felt her chest rising and falling, the silk sliding subtly against her breasts with each breath, his eyes watching with scarcely disguised longing. "I don't know if they look funny on," she continued. "I didn't notice them last night."

One sable eyebrow arched. "Is that a hint?"

"You might take it that way," she agreed. "But be forewarned. I might laugh."

"Oh, really?" He shook his head and released her. "Then forget it. Hurry up and get dressed, or we'll miss the tip-off."

She rose up on her elbows, her eyes narrowed. "You're right. It's not every day you get to see Isiah Thomas."

Jeff started to stand, but she reached out and grabbed his arm.

"Jeff, you don't want to go to the game, do you?"

"Sure I do."

"You didn't even know the Mavs were playing the Lakers, the biggest game of the season so far. Jeff, do you know anything about basketball at all?"

"Of course I do. Two baskets, five players, bounce the ball, no traveling, no tackling, no spitting."

"All of which you learned in school. Tell me, who's the starting guard for the Mavericks?"

He shot her a dirty look.

She leaned back against the wall, feeling rather smug. "It was a dead giveaway when you didn't remind me that Isiah Thomas is a Piston, not a Laker or a Mav. Piston, as in Detroit."

"What's the point of all this?" Jeff asked, exasperated. "Is this some further proof that I'm—"

"I won't laugh."

"You won't— Oh? Oh, really. You're going to miss your game," he said thoughtfully, watching her.

"Not if I play it right." She giggled again. "At least, not the game I'm thinking of."

"Cecilia, you're crazy."

"I know," she agreed happily. "And I don't even wear plaid underwear."

"You're not going to let it drop, are you?"

"What color are you wearing today? Polka dot? No, white with red hearts."

"Cecilia," he explained patiently, "polka dots and red hearts have no class."

"Plaid does," she remarked neutrally.

"In my opinion."

She measured her words carefully, enjoying the flavor of them on her lips. "Prove it."

He drew a deep breath, his eyelids lowering.

She leaned forward, propping her elbows on her knees, her chin on her fists.

"What kind of wanton woman have I allowed into my domain?" he asked accusingly as he rose to his full height.

"I believe the correct term is 'brazen hussy.'"

"I stand corrected." The belt buckle clicked free, then he slid the belt out and dropped it on the floor.

Cecilia closed her eyes and swallowed. What had gotten into her? She opened them again, and he was sliding his chinos down his thighs. He dropped to the piano stool; it squeaked in protest. He tugged first one leg, then the other, free.

Red plaid.

She caught her lower lip with her teeth.

"Don't you dare," he threatened.

"They're not . . . they're not classy, Jeff."

"All right," he growled. "Go ahead. Get it over with."

"They're . . ." She almost choked on the word. "They're sexy as hell."

A slow stain crept over his cheeks, and she ducked her head. "Well, you asked!"

"Cecilia, I feel ridiculous."

"They're your shorts."

"That's not what I mean. I mean, pulling off my trousers just so you can see my boxers."

She raised her head and met his gaze. "You mean . . . you mean, that's the only reason you took them off?"

Nine

In three strides Jeff crossed the room to scoop Cecilia, twisting and giggling, from the floor and into his arms. "You're driving me crazy, woman," he growled. He nudged the door open wider with his shoulder and carried her through.

"Put me down!" She kicked her legs as he headed down the hall to the bedroom. "Ow!" she howled. "I kicked the wall!"

"Serves you right. You're going to pay for this."

Then his head dipped and his mouth went unerringly to the gaping spot on her—his—shirt. He buried his face in the soft flesh of her stomach and nibbled, tickling her unmercifully. Her howl turned into a squeal. "Jeff! Stop! I-I—" She twisted in his arms, but he was relentless, and she laughed and cried and laughed harder, until she was gasping for air.

"Ticklish?" he drawled, and she felt his shoulders flex, his arms tense, as he released her over the bed and, laughing, watched her fall.

Her body left her stomach behind a split second before she hit the bed, and it took a good three seconds for her stomach to catch up. "You—you're a maniac!" Cecilia gasped.

"I beg your pardon," Jeff said, tugging his shirt over his head. He grabbed her from behind when she started to squirm off the other side of the bed. "Not so fast." As effortlessly as if she were a bag of feathers, he draped an arm across her and pinned her down while, with his free hand, he pulled his socks off, one after the other. "Now repeat after me, 'I will never laugh at plaid underwear again.'"

"Good grief," she groaned, rolling her eyes, and attempted to wiggle free.

"No, no," he chided. "You haven't learned your lesson. Now repeat after me. 'I will never laugh at plaid underwear again.'"

"You're despicable."

"No. As a matter of fact, when I consider the hell you put me through all those long years ago, I think you've deserved this for a long time." His fingers skimmed down her side and she flinched and squeaked and arched away from them.

"Stop it!"

"'I won't laugh at plaid underwear ever again,'" he repeated sternly, this time his tongue finding the sensitive spot behind her ear.

She sighed, relieved. More than relieved.

"Nope. Wrong reaction," he apologized, and snatched her arm, the better to tickle the inside of her elbow, the soft underside of her upper arm and then higher—

"I won't laugh at plaid underwear ev—ever again!" she screeched, then collapsed, limp, when he pulled back and grinned.

"There. Was that so difficult?"

"Damn you. Damn you, Jefferson Smith."

He shook his head sadly. "I'm afraid so, Cecil. And you did it." He bent closer, found her lips clamped shut against him, and teased them to soft compliance.

"If...if you really must," she grumbled, straining to keep some semblance of irritation in her voice, "could you please turn on the radio?"

Giving her a lazy, superior look, he reached for the bedside table and hit at the On button of the radio, missed, but still didn't trust her enough to release her. The third attempt was the charm, as music filled the room.

"'Meaner than a junkyard dog...'"

"Oh, give me strength," she groaned. "Not Leroy Brown."

Jeff hooted with laughter. "Yes, Cecil, most definitely Leroy Brown." His lips captured hers again, and she didn't try quite so hard to avoid them. "I think..." he whispered into her ear, "I think I left something in my pocket."

Cecilia craned her neck to see what could possibly be so important, and spied the pocketless polo shirt on the floor.

"Not that one." Jeff's fingers delved into the pocket of his silk shirt, and she gasped. Her nipple's hard, pebbled surface ricocheted with sensation as his fingers rubbed it. "Ah, yes, Cecil...I found it."

"Oh...my." She sank into the mattress, giving up completely. She didn't have the strength or the desire to fight. Besides, there were times when surrender was so much more rewarding.

"Did you say something?" he asked.

"'Oh...my.'" She glared up at him. "I believe you've heard it before."

"Eloquently, my dear. Eloquently." Under his expert tutelage, her other breast learned to quiver at the touch of silk and knowing fingertips, and then of moist warmth as he captured it with his mouth, his tongue, until it pressed against the wet silk in roseate splendor. "Are you...learning your lesson?" he rasped.

"I don't know whether to hit you for being a jerk," she moaned, "or...or..."

"I definitely prefer the 'or.'" He popped the shirt buttons open one by one and spread the shirt. The cool air hit her, tightening the flesh around her sensitized nipples. The eyes he raised to her were filled with awe, with amazement. "You are so beautiful."

"Don't say—"

"I will say it." He moved over her, smoothing her curls away from her face, holding her cheeks between his palms

to keep her from turning away. "You have to listen to me,
Cecilia. You are so full of something...bubbly. I can't de-
scribe it, except to say it's you. If someone were to bottle
champagne in a woman, it would be in you. In your voice,
in your eyes, in your laughter, in the way you wiggle when
you walk." He placed a kiss on her eyelids tenderly, teas-
ingly. "That's as poetic as I know how to be, and every word
of it is God's honest truth."

Something in her blossomed, aching and new, something
she didn't dare name, something she had to deny at all costs.
"You're quite good at this, you know," she said weakly.

He took the fingers that twined in his hair and freed them,
kissing their tips, taking the smallest one into his mouth and
sucking gently with teeth and tongue. "I believe anything
worth doing is worth doing well," he promised ardently.
"It's part of my nature."

And she believed him. Oh, my, did she believe him. She
believed him from the tingles in her toes to the tightening
between her legs. She believed him when his eyes loved her
with liquid brown warmth. She believed him when his lips
whispered sweet nothings that echoed meaninglessly, yet
were fraught with meaning.

She gasped, arched, trembled when his fingers slipped
between her thighs and probed, found, stroked. Her legs
were leaden; her hands clenched restlessly as he built and
nurtured that lovely ache. She heard the whimper escaping
her lips, as did he, and he kissed her, capturing her sounds
of desperation and making them his. His tongue stroked,
matching the rhythmic assault of his fingers and filling her
with languid desire. The erotic tension mounted in her with
an urgency demanding release. She slid her trembling hands
down his body, found him, felt him throbbing with need for
her, and guided him into her, to a tumultuous response that
started, for her, almost before he was snugly sheathed.

Her lips trembled, her body convulsed around him, as he
moved slowly, deliberately, bringing her to a place she'd
never known before and driving her over the edge. She was
on fire, her veins filled with shimmering, molten silver as she
writhed beneath him, found his shoulder and pressed her
mouth against it to keep from crying out, to keep from

crying.... The tears were lodged in her throat, and she swallowed them back, gulping, gasping, until she couldn't move, and still he filled her, still he held back, patiently, oh, so patiently.

She lay beneath him, shaken, almost destroyed by the knowledge of what this man could do to her that had never been done before. She'd shared loving experiences, but she'd never been totally and completely loved; she had never had every nuance of her reactions painstakingly responded to by someone more intent on her pleasure than his own. And it was more than that. She'd never felt so vulnerable, so emotionally naked. She was numb. She was terrified.

His shoulders were rock beneath her kneading hands, the imprint of her teeth white against tan. Stricken with guilt, she raised her head to kiss, to apologize with actions because she had no words. She tasted the salt of his skin as she tried to soothe away the marks of her passion. Her thighs wrapped him more tightly, her hands stroked down his taut back, and even when she thought to do so would shatter her, she began to move against him, building his heat with her friction. She had to give what she could, even while she was painfully aware of what she couldn't.

She could make no promises for tomorrow, but neither could she allow room for doubts about now. Now was theirs, hers to give to him as much as he'd given to her.

Every nerve ending was jagged sensation pushed beyond endurance, and yet she more than endured, she gloried in the feel of him driving, shaking, shuddering, and then arching, burying himself in her with a cry no effort could stifle.

"Hold me," he whispered into her shoulder. "Hold me."

And she clung, because to let go was to lose him. To let go was to lose now. And now was all they had.

"Did I hurt you?" he asked when his fingers found her cheeks damp.

"No," she whispered. *But you will. You will....* Where were the bubbles? His heat had boiled them out of her. She didn't feel there was any laughter left in her, so intense was the response he had pulled from her.

"Don't leave, Cecilia," he murmured against her. "Stay with me tonight."

She stroked his temple with fingers that had soothed a thousand hurts. "I have to go home."

An hour later Jeff stood by helplessly as Cecilia scurried up the stairs for the fourth time, disappeared into the spare room, came out again. "What are you looking for?" he asked again.

She shook her head. "Nothing. Just making sure I don't leave anything."

He had supplied her with the only apparel he could come up with that even came close to being appropriate. In the midday light, her skin was pale against his old University of Texas T-shirt and faded orange cotton gym shorts. Her dress, shoes and stockings were in the brown bag she clutched in her hand. Her eyes were large and dark in her pale face. Even her freckles seemed to have been swallowed up by her pallor. She acted as if she felt displaced.

His arms ached to encircle her again. His hands wanted to seek the tangled confusion of her hair. He wanted to pull her into his lap and convince her the world hadn't ended just because she was going home. He wanted to believe it himself.

She waited by the door, hardly seeming to notice him as she stared into the living room, at the newspapers that were now stacked neatly beside his chair, at the stereo system that played his jazz.

And then her gaze landed on Toulouse. Her eyebrows met in a frown. She stepped up to the bird. Toulouse ruffled his neck feathers and lowered his head, aiming his orange glare at her.

Before Jeff could stop her, she offered the bird her hand, one red oval nail pointing at him. After a moment's angry contemplation, the bird struck with a squawk and a beating of wings.

Cecilia jerked her hand back but stood firmly in front of the perch. Jeff lunged forward, his hand raised. "I ought to—"

She grabbed his wrist, her blood hot and wet, bonding them. "No. It's not his fault."

He clasped her hand. "Why did you—Cecilia, what were you thinking of?" He pulled out a handkerchief to stanch the flow of blood. "For pete's sake, why?"

She watched him work on her finger without flinching. "I thought maybe if I met him halfway..."

Jeff shook his head, confused. "What's wrong, Cecil?"

She ran her uninjured hand through her hair, brushing it out of her face, avoiding his eyes. "I'm tired, that's all. I need to go home."

He didn't want to let go of her hand. He didn't want to let her leave. He touched her face, tracing her cheek, her jaw, then placed a curled finger under her chin and gently forced her to look at him. Her eyes shimmered; her lower lip quivered. "Cecilia, something has happened between us, and I don't know what."

"I can't talk about it now."

"Whatever it is, promise me we'll talk about it later."

She glanced away, then back again.

"Don't shut me out, Cecil."

She smiled tremulously and he felt the tightness in his middle lessen.

She raised her bound finger between them. "I might sue your lousy bird."

He tweaked her chin. "How about an out-of-court settlement?"

"Maybe..." Her smile took on a devious glint. "And there's also the matter of you making me miss the hottest basketball game of the season."

"What do you want from me? Blood?" He chuckled.

"Blood doesn't work." She grimaced, then her expression sobered. "How about you meeting Peter halfway?"

The question was casual, yet he could feel her tension. "Halfway to Peter is still a long, long way." She stiffened. Damn it, she couldn't even tell he was teasing. He had to try a little harder. "And I'm not sure it's worth the trip."

Her chin snapped up and she glared at him.

"But to avoid a lawsuit, I suppose I could try."

He watched the realization that he was teasing slowly come over her, the cautious relief wipe the strain from her expression. "Of course," she said dryly. "What other reason would there be?"

Peter. The kid hated him. Jeff felt a little as though he had dodged a bullet and then walked straight into a spray of machine-gun fire.

He gave her a quick hug. "Let's get you home and into clean clothes so we can work out the details."

When they pulled up in front of Cecilia's house, a black Mercedes was parked in the driveway. Jeff saw her glance guiltily at her clothes.

"What's up?" he asked.

"I don't know. The kids were supposed to be with Robert all weekend. They'd actually been looking forward to it for a change. Robert was taking them to the zoo today and fishing tomorrow." Her hands clenched in her lap. "I hope nothing's happened."

She slammed the door as she got out. Jeff winced. She was halfway across the yard before he caught up with her. "It's okay," he murmured, grabbing her elbow.

"Why, Cecilia, there you are." Monica stood poised in the arched doorway. "Robert got called to Odessa. Business, you know."

Oh, yes, I know, she said to herself. "I hope you made yourself at home."

Jeff found himself wondering how she could sound so casual, so welcoming.

"The kids are out back. I guess now that you're here, I'll go on."

"Thanks for staying with them." Cecilia stopped in the hallway and waited by the door while Monica gathered her purse and paperback.

Jeff stood by the stairs, out of the line of fire.

"How long have y'all been here?" Cecilia asked.

"Three hours. When Robert asked me to drop them off, he assumed you'd be home." She glanced significantly from Cecilia to Jeff. "Obviously he was wrong."

"I hope the children weren't any problem."

"That Peter is such a sweetheart. You hardly know he's there. He's an intelligent child, isn't he?" Monica said. Her perfectly arched eyebrows met in a slight frown. "I suppose the others will mature nicely, given time."

Jeff stood straighter. "Yes, those two are delightful little scamps, aren't they?"

He didn't know who seemed more startled, Monica or Cecilia. He slipped his arm around Cecilia's shoulders. "Especially Ann-Elizabeth. But, then, she takes after her mother."

"Oh, yes." Monica rubbed her upper arm. "I've noticed."

She left with little further ado, and only then did Jeff finally allow himself the luxury of laughter. "Can you see her trying to handle those kids by herself for three hours? It's a wonder the house is still standing."

Cecilia's icy glare hit him full force. "What else would you expect?"

Ouch. He followed her to the screened back porch. The children didn't hear them approach. Anne-Elizabeth's squeals pierced the air.

"Giddyap!" Anne-Elizabeth clutched Peter's wiry shoulders and neck as he galloped across the lush green lawn. "Faster!" she cried, bouncing on his back.

Peter accommodated her, his thin legs pumping. They rounded a tree and came back.

Brad seemed unaffected as they raced by him. He simply kept juggling his soccer ball. "Thirty-one." Off his knee. "Thirty-two." Off his other knee. "Thirty-three— Oh, shoot!" The ball glanced off his toe and sailed into the bushes, where Ralph lay, his long tongue hanging out. Brad looked up and saw his mother.

"Mom! I set a new record! Thirty-three times without touching the ground! Didja see me?" He bounded toward them, his red hair glinting in the sunlight.

Peter stopped, heaving for breath, and his sister slid off his back to the ground. "Mommy!"

By the time Peter caught up, Cecilia was hugging her squirming, squealing, sweating children.

"Where were you?" Brad asked. "We waited forever!"

At that moment, Peter looked up and saw Jeff. He looked back at his mother, at her clothing. "Shut up, Brad."

"But where—"

"Let's get something to drink." Cecilia grabbed Peter by one hand and her daughter by the other. "Get your ball, Brad, before Ralph buries it. We'll fix lemonade."

"Those were neat pictures you took," Brad said as they ambled toward the house. "I stuck 'em on my bulletin board, except the one where I was in the middle of the air." Brad tucked the soccer ball under his arm and smiled up at Jeff. "That one looked real neat, like Tatu, or somethin'. I gave it to my dad, 'cause he hardly ever gets to go to my games. Even Monica said she liked it, even though she was still mad at me for breakin' the lamp."

Jeff stopped. "You broke a lamp?"

"It wasn't my fault. I was jugglin' and Anne-Elizabeth bumped into me, and when we crashed the ball kinda went wild." The impish grin on his face showed he felt little remorse. "Monica went crazy."

"I can well imagine," Jeff said sternly.

Brad shrugged. "She's stupid. She only likes Peter 'cause he doesn't cause any trouble. She thinks me and Anne-Elizabeth are demons. She said so the first time we ever went over there, just 'cause Annie cried at night when Monica tried to tuck her in, and she wanted to go home and wouldn't let my dad near her, and I snuck off and called Mom. Monica said we were trying to make her look bad."

"And what did Peter do during all this?" Jeff asked, morbidly interested in spite of himself.

"He *apologized*. He told Monica Annie and me were just upset. He's the biggest fake."

"What do you mean?"

"By the time Mom got there, he'd already packed our bags and acted all like the boss, and Dad said he was proud of him for bein' the one in charge...and then as soon as we got in the car he started bawlin' just like me an' Anne-Elizabeth." Brad kicked a large red rock, and it made a heavy scuttering sound as it rolled down the walk.

"What did your mom do?" Jeff asked quietly.

Brad stood still for a minute, frowning. Suddenly his face lit up. "Oh, yeah! That was the night she took us to Uncle Stan's, and he let us play. I played the drums and Annie played the keyboard and Peter played the electric guitar— It was awful!" He burst into giggles. "Then we went to Burger Barn—they're open till after midnight! That was neat." Suddenly his face fell. "And the next day she made us all apologize, all except Annie, 'cause she was too little, and Peter had already apologized, so that meant me. Just me. I told Monica I was sorry and—and—" He turned a disgusted face up to Jeff. "She kissed me! She left big fat red lips marks on my face. It was gross!"

Anne-Elizabeth burst through the door. "Mommy said come in!" She whirled and ran back, without pausing to see if they followed.

When Jeff entered the kitchen, the pitcher of lemonade was on the counter, Peter was nowhere to be seen and Cecilia seemed upset.

"What's wrong?" Jeff asked.

"I thought maybe Carol would take me back over to your place so I could pick up my car, but nobody's home over there."

"I can take you back. What's the problem?"

"I can't just go off and leave the kids."

"Of course you can't." He tried to hide the strain he was under, tried to make his voice casual. "They'll go with us. What's the big deal?"

"But your car is so small," she began, but Brad broke in.

"It's not too small. Me and Peter and Anne-Elizabeth can squeeze in the back seat." He turned to Jeff. "Is the top down?"

Jeff nodded, and Brad let out a shout. He ran toward the front door, calling his brother and sister. "Come on, we're going to Jeff's!"

"Brad!" Jeff called, and the boy stopped just short of a collision with a lamp table. "The ball stays here."

Jeff watched as Brad tossed it and bounced it off his head, following it with a cocky grin as it landed in an easy chair. "Okay."

Maybe his apartment would survive....

Late that night, Cecilia sat alone on the front porch swing. She had wrapped herself in a faded old quilt, the fabric and stitches of a great-grandmother she'd never known. They offered her no comfort, not tonight.

One weekend had come and gone and somehow shattered her warm, untidy little world into a thousand frightening pieces. She didn't want to quiver with need for a man's touch. She didn't want to find a man's presence so comforting....

Damn it, Jeff had been wrong for her all those years ago. How dared he come into her life and seem so right for her now? How dared he look into her heart and pronounce so analytically and understandingly that the goals she'd set for herself were wrong?

How dared he understand her better than she'd been understanding herself lately?

But the most shattering effect of their time together was the knowledge that she would go back for more. She couldn't turn her back on what he offered. She couldn't deny herself the pleasure of his company, the aching response to his touch.

Perhaps there was a satisfactory solution: to share and enjoy without possessing or needing. Surely they were mature enough for that. After all, Jeff couldn't want the shackles of a permanent relationship with her any more than she wanted one with him.

The swing creaked and she smiled in spite of herself, remembering ... chocolate and raspberry ice cream, a black feather boa, red tartan boxer shorts.

At least their relationship wouldn't be boring.

The boys were in school and Anne-Elizabeth was playing army next door with Vinny. Cecilia had nothing more pressing than a dirty kitchen to keep her mind off Jeff.

Fat chance. She turned her back on the mess and drifted into the bedroom. Over the past eight weeks, no matter how demanding her schedule, nothing had kept her mind off Jeff for longer than ten minutes at a time, if that long.

Sitting in the studio this morning, a word, a single word uttered by a sound technician, had brought Jeff into full-blown, Cinemascope focus, and she'd stuttered, messing up the opening to an advertising jingle for a national fried chicken franchise. Three times.

Cecilia grabbed a laundry basket and carried it into her bedroom, then dropped to the floor, prepared to sort socks and underwear. She flipped the radio onto a classic rock station and closed her eyes, letting the gentle syncopation of an old Doobie Brothers tune flow through her. The attic fan sucked a steady draft of warm, honeysuckle-scented May air through the open window beside her, and the sun shone through the sheer lace curtains and cast a dimpling gold glaze over her. She felt lazy. Tired, but nicely so.

Jeff had stayed late the night before. They had talked quietly on the porch swing, with the first fireflies dancing on the lawn. The kids had been upstairs asleep, yet other than nestling against him, she had not allowed herself the luxury of kisses and caresses. Kisses and caresses might lead to far more than she was comfortable with under the same roof with her children. Yet when he finally left, the kiss he gave her had been potent with hunger, so potent she had been at the brink of asking him inside, when he had pulled away abruptly and given her the saddest of moonlit smiles to haunt her for the rest of the night.

Alone in the darkness, it was the sadness, the longing, that had permeated her with a slow, throbbing ache. She didn't want to kiss him good-night at the door and spend the long and lonely nights alone like a lovesick teenager. Her heart was that of a woman, selfish enough to want him completely, and damn the consequences.

Consequences. What a simple, generic term for two little boys, a little girl, a dog and a bird...not to mention conflicting life-styles from A to Z. She knew that Jeff's tendency to pick up her towels even before they hit the floor could get old fast. They had discovered during their rare weekends at his apartment that while she woke up singing and happily clattering around in the kitchen, Jeff was more inclined to growl and cover up his head. How would he survive mornings with squealing and laughter and a game of hide-and-seek that would end up under her bed, more likely than not. He didn't even appreciate the breakfast omelets with chilies, onions and cheese, which were her specialty, nor did she appreciate his obsession with keeping every receipt filed, every mile logged, every item in a checkbook balanced and accounted for....

"An accountant," she groaned. "How did I ever let myself go and fall in love with an accountant?"

She sat up so abruptly she knocked over the basket of clothes.

"I didn't say that," she announced loudly to the floral wallpaper. But the thumping of her heart and the spasm in her stomach announced just as loudly that whether or not she had said it, she had meant it. She sprang to her feet.

"I love him." The world didn't crumble around her head, but it might as well have. "Oh, God," she moaned, clenching her fists to her temples. "I do, I do. I love him." And then, as shock and frustration overcame the initial astonishment, she grabbed a pillow off the bed and hurled it at the ceiling. It landed on her head, then bounced to the floor. "How could you?" she demanded, meeting her own angry glare in the mottled mirror over her antique oak dresser. "How could you do this to me?"

She fell back on the bed, fighting tears, then laughter when Ralph launched himself onto the bed beside her, determined to tend his mistress's needs whether they be a strong warm shoulder to cry on or a clean face. Holding him at arms length, she grew thoughtful. "There's one problem we could eliminate in a hurry." She drew closer, staring at his big brown eyes with evil intent. "Ralphie...have you ever eaten a bird?"

April 15 was six weeks past, but quarter filings should have been occupying Jeff's time. Instead he shot a rubber band at McVay as she disappeared through the closing door. It struck the doorjamb and bounced harmlessly to the floor, but only because he'd intended it to.

"Are my habits so cast in stone that if I vary them it merits a press release?" he called after her irritably, but she merely shut the door between them.

All he'd done was to tell her he was leaving early, and she'd looked at him as if she were contemplating calling the men in white coats. The same way Fiona had looked at him when he'd given her a hamburger franchise freebie—a red-haired clown doll—to give to her little girl.

What was wrong with everybody?

Did everyone see him as some kind of stodgy, boring accountant? For pete's sake, he even wore paisley suspenders. He ran his thumbs under them to reassure himself. It was only that Cecilia's quirkiness, her haphazardness, made him feel stodgy by comparison. Normal women found him, well, maybe a little conservative, but charming. Attractive. Generous. They'd told him so, and more than one had tried to seal their relationship with a very conservative marital knot.

But no one had ever, ever found him sexy as hell, except Cecilia.

How could he be satisfied with a comfortable, sensible relationship with an efficient, attractive woman? He'd been looking for someone who'd be obsessed with him, who'd make him feel like the most desirable, exciting man in the world, even when he knew different. Maybe subconsciously he'd been searching for another Cecil…and, heaven help him, he'd rediscovered the original.

But with the rediscovery, he'd learned something even more frightening: that he could share that obsession, could be driven to distraction by his need for her, his love for her, his determination to make everything right for her. He buried his face in his hands in frustration.

Her life was so damned complete. Sure, he was part of it, but only the most expendable part. It wasn't that she made him feel unwanted. Somehow she managed to bestow the same obsessive energy on everything—her work, her children, her life—and still have plenty left for him. He'd like to think he was responsible for the fact that her energy seemed purer now, less strained, less compulsive than when they'd first started seeing each other. She definitely needed him, but she needed him in the corners of her life, not in the middle of it. And that's where he wanted to be, damn it. In the middle.

In the middle of all that chaos?

He shuddered. Everything seemed to have its price, and his sanity was beginning to seem a small price to pay for her joy and radiance. When analyzed singly, he thought the chaos was manageable. Anne-Elizabeth truly was the image of her mother, and therefore totally lovable, despite her prickly edges. Brad, too, possessed Cecilia's buoyancy, her enthusiasm, her cocky self-assurance. Despite his loud, boyish clamorings, Brad could be a perfectly enchanting child.

Peter, on the other hand, was quite another subject. Meet him halfway, Cecilia had said. The farther Jeff stretched, the tighter Peter coiled. Jeff had attempted a discussion of the merits of IBC as compared to Digitox computer hardware, hoping to meet Peter on common ground. He should have known that since his own office was totally IBC, Peter would have voiced a decided preference for Digitox. What could have been a shared interest quickly escalated into a battle, with both parties retiring to their corners to sulk. Yes, he admitted it, he'd sulked. The kid actually knew more about computers than he did.

To make matters worse, the day the kids had been at his apartment that damned Toulouse had traitorously decided to like the kid. After going absolutely berserk at the sight of Cecilia and Anne-Elizabeth, the bird had turned into a fluttering ball of excitement at the sight of Peter. Within five minutes the parrot had been riding on Peter's shoulder and calling the kid "Harry." The fact that Peter's cottony-white hair and glasses were similar in color and style to Uncle Harry's did little to assuage Jeff's hurt pride. Heck, when he had first inherited the bird, it had taken him two weeks just to get the bird to eat, and another month before the bird would allow him to stroke its head.

Halfway to Peter was a still a long way, but Jeff admitted grudgingly that his own attitudes could stand a little adjusting. Surely there was some common ground they could meet on. Unfortunately the only common ground he could think of was Cecilia. Peter adored his mother. So did Jeff. And that "common ground" was obviously a battleground.

But the thought of Cecilia, even in the context of her son, was still enough to bring a wistful smile to Jeff's lips. When it came to Cecilia, his sanity was a small price to pay, indeed.

He flipped through the telephone directory and began making calls. The third was the charm. He hung up the telephone with a satisfied sigh, refusing to be dismayed by the expense of his plan. If he was going to fit into the chaos, it was time to start trying a little harder.

He picked up the phone again and buzzed McVay.

"You're still here?" she asked.

"I'm leaving now, but be forewarned, I'm leaving early next Monday and Wednesday."

"Jeff, is something wrong? You certainly haven't been yourself lately."

"Is that bad?" he asked, curious.

"No." She paused. "No, now that you mention it, that's not bad at all."

"Well, then," he said with a laugh, suddenly feeling a little giddy, "I guess nothing's wrong."

He tossed a wad of paper at the wastepaper basket and missed, slung his suit jacket over his shoulder and walked through the door whistling "Bad, Bad Leroy Brown."

Ten

Cecilia bustled from Anne-Elizabeth's room, her arms full of dirty clothes and linens.

"Mom," Brad grumbled, tagging along. "I don't think you should let her wear that shirt."

"We've been over this a hundred times, Brad. Anne-Elizabeth is not being deliberately disloyal." She stepped on an all-too-familiar hard object on the bottom step and kicked it aside before taking the next step. "Pick up that car," she ordered.

Brad scooped it up but wasn't about to let the subject change. "But Mom, ya didn't have to let her have a Lakers shirt! I don't care if it is purple!"

"Sweetheart," Cecilia explained with a sigh, "when a little girl refuses to wear anything but purple, you'll take anything purple you can get. Why else would she have four TCU Horned Frog T-shirts? It's called desperation!"

Peter raised his head from an Agatha Christie mystery as they entered the kitchen. He closed his book. "The judge did it."

"Are you finished already?" she asked, tousling his hair.

"Nope. But just remember that when I got to page thirty-seven, I'd already figured it out."

"All right. Figure this out." Cecilia had been saving this trick for a week. She grabbed a piece of paper and drew a rectangle, then printed the name "GATEMAN" in the center. "It's a palindrome."

"What's a palindrome?" Brad asked, crossing over to look.

"Dummy," Peter muttered without malice, intent on his mother's puzzle. "A palindrome is a word or a phrase that reads the same backward and forward."

"Mommy!" Anne-Elizabeth burst into the kitchen. "Jeff's here. He bwought a su'pwize!"

Cecilia's heart did a double beat in her chest as she looked past Ann-Elizabeth. "Where is he, honey?"

"On the porch."

"Why didn't he come in?"

"Oops." Anne-Elizabeth's pudgy hand covered her rosy lips and her eyes were even bigger than usual. "I forgot to wet him in." She immediately whirled and took off, the loose purple strings in her red high-tops flapping with each step.

"I don't get it," Brad said.

Moments later Anne-Elizabeth reappeared, and this time Jeff was towering behind her, a hesitant grin on his face. "Hi."

"Hi." Cecilia smoothed her blouse over her capri pants and smiled. "I wasn't expecting you tonight."

"I have a surprise." His eyes were positively glowing.

"I don't get it," Brad repeated, a little louder.

Peter's attention remained deliberately concentrated on the paper in front of him.

"A surprise?" Cecilia asked.

"No," Brad insisted. "A palindrome. I still don't get it."

Jeff seemed a little frustrated that his "surprise" wasn't gathering any more attention than it was, but Cecilia just shook her head apologetically. "Hold it. Let me straighten this out. Watch this, Brad." She took another piece of paper and wrote across it "Toby Harrah."

"The baseball player," Brad said.

She drew a line through his first name. "Spell 'Harrah" backward.

"*H-A-R-R-A-H*." Brad's frown cleared. "Oh, I get it! The same backward and forward!" He raised his freckled face to Jeff. "'Toby Harrah' is a palindrome!"

"Does he get paid extra for that?" Jeff asked dryly.

"Get lost," Peter muttered, without looking up.

"I wanna be a palindwome," Anne-Elizabeth squealed. "Spell me backward!"

"Beth-Eliza-Anne," Jeff responded promptly, squatting beside her, and Annie giggled her delight. Peter stared resolutely at the puzzle.

Brad bent over his paper, frowning. Suddenly his head shot up. "I got one!"

"What?" Cecilia leaned over his shoulder and choked.

"'Tit'! 'Tit' is a palindrome!"

"Bradley Davis Evans!" she gasped, holding back her laughter.

"Very good," Jeff said. "And a very nice one at that."

"Jeff, don't encourage him." The washing machine went into the spin cycle and began walking across the floor. "Hold it." Cecilia opened the lid. Just as she'd expected, the large wad of lavender sheets was pressed on one side of the machine's interior. Anne-Elizabeth's purple shirts didn't begin to balance the load on the other side. Cecilia grabbed a fistful of sopping sheet and began redistributing the load. When she closed the lid and turned the machine back on, she glanced up to see Jeff watching her every move with amused indulgence.

"Chaos," he said, then grinned.

"What a jerk." Peter's comment was nearly inaudible.

"Takes one to know one," Jeff retorted, reaching into his pocket.

"Jeff," Cecilia said warily, "are you feeling okay?"

"Terrific. Now is anyone at all interested in my surprise?"

"Mom, I give up." Peter shoved the paper away, to Cecilia's utter amazement. Peter never ever gave up on anything. She glanced at Jeff and saw his frustrated expression as he held an envelope in his hands, and knew Peter's motivation.

"That's all right, darling. Now let's see what kind of surprise Jeff has."

But Jeff seemed to reconsider, and slid the envelope back in his pocket. "Let me see what you gave up on."

Peter was reaching to pull the sheet of paper back, when Brad snatched it away and thrust it at Jeff. "You figure it out! I'll bet you can't."

Jeff studied the rectangle and the name, his forehead creased in a frown.

Cecilia hoped she didn't look as smug as she felt. It wasn't every day she could outthink Jeff and Peter in one fell swoop.

"Give 'em a hint," Brad said.

Peter glowered; Jeff continued to frown.

"Myron Rhodentucker had one." With that Cecilia swept from the room, the sweet taste of victory almost as thrilling as Jeff's unexpected visit. She dropped onto the sofa in the living room and tucked her bare feet beneath her, and waited.

It didn't take long. Jeff appeared in the doorway with a triumphant grin. Anne-Elizabeth leaned comfortably against his leg as she nibbled on a celery stick, and Brad strained eagerly to see the paper in Jeff's hand. Finally Peter followed them, his pale face set in sullen lines.

"You think you've got it?" Cecilia asked, idly examining her manicure.

"I know I do." Jeff produced the puzzle's solution with a flourish. "It's a name tag. Gateman's name tag. Spelled the same backward and forward."

Peter snatched the paper away from him and studied it for a long moment. He raised his face to his mother's and his eyes were hurt, accusing. "You...that wasn't fair," he said. "You gave him a hint that I wouldn't understand."

Cecilia felt herself flush with chagrin. "It was only a game, Peter."

"But you helped him." He didn't need to finish what he was thinking. Cecilia saw it written in the pained confusion on his face: *You helped him beat me.*

She sprang from the sofa and crossed to put her arms around him. "I'm sorry," she said. "You're right. It wasn't fair." She felt his hard, thin shoulders refuse to relax against her, and felt a pang of guilt.

"I want my su'pwize," Anne-Elizabeth demanded, tired of games she didn't understand.

Jeff seemed to relax a bit. "Coming right up," he said, and dropped down beside her. He reached into his pocket and pulled out the envelope once again. He extracted several oblong folders. "Take your pick, milady."

She fingered the corner of first one, then another, unable to make up her mind.

"Come on, let me," Brad said, reaching.

"Nope," Jeff said, blocking his hand. "Ladies first."

So of course Anne-Elizabeth took extra time studying the folders, which she couldn't read, while Brad bounced from one foot to another behind her. Finally she pulled one out and opened it, bemused.

"Next?" Jeff offered his hand to Brad, and he grabbed one. Before Jeff could even offer Peter a chance, Brad was screaming at the top of his lungs, "Playoff tickets! Mom, he got tickets to the Mavs' home games next week!"

"What?" Cecilia grabbed a folder. "Good gravy, Jeff! Where on earth did you—why, you must have paid a fortune! Both games? I can't believe it."

"It's all a matter of knowing who to call," Jeff responded humbly, pressing a folder of tickets into Peter's hand. "And if there's a game six, we'll be there, too."

Cecilia looked into his velvety brown eyes and saw such pride, such pleasure, it brought a warm glow to her insides. "You shouldn't have," she murmured.

"I thought the kids would be pleased," he said. "Besides, I owe you a Lakers game, don't I?"

"Wakers?" Anne-Elizabeth asked, her face suddenly brightening.

Brad stopped celebrating long enough to stare at his mother in horror. "You aren't gonna let her wear—"

"That's my fav'wite shirt." Anne-Elizabeth beamed.

"Oh, Mom," Brad groaned. "I'll die. I'll just die." He aimed a fierce scowl at his sister. "If she wears that shirt, I'll kill her."

"You will not kill your sister," Cecilia responded firmly. "Annie, why don't you let me buy you a pretty new green shirt?"

Anne-Elizabeth set her full lips into a firm line and shook her head violently.

"Blue?"

Again, belligerent refusal.

"A new purple one, without letters or numbers on it. Plain and pretty?"

This time Anne-Elizabeth gave a reluctant nod. "All wight."

It was then that Cecilia noticed Peter—or rather, she noticed that he had left without saying a word. His tickets were on the floor. Jeff stooped to pick them up, his frustration evident in the set of his shoulders, the way his eyebrows met in a tense, straight line.

"Don't worry. I'll talk to him," Cecilia said. But somehow she knew that Peter would be more difficult to reason with than her daughter. There were some hurts a new purple shirt just couldn't begin to fix.

Like having your mother help someone else make you look dumb.

She closed her eyes against the strain. How could she make him see that he and Jeff weren't in a contest and that she wasn't the prize?

Saturday morning at 7:00 Cecilia closed the front door behind her and leaned against it, yawning. She'd worked late the night before, then gotten the kids off to the airport at dawn for their flight to San Antonio. Even though Robert and Monica had seemed to have everything under control, she hadn't left Love Field until the commercial jet was aloft and out of sight. She carried the newspaper into the living room and sank to the floor, hoping to see how her favorite sports columnist viewed the Mavs' chances against the Lakers.

A dreadful country and western rendition of "Don't Be Cruel" was blaring on the radio. She switched on the turntable and searched for a record, something soothing. She had hours, blessed hours, alone before Jeff was coming, and all she wanted to do was relax.

A Simon and Garfunkel album was on the top of the stack. She grabbed it and put it on, just to break the silence while she looked for something more... She sighed. More what? Humming along to "Punky's Dilemma," she flipped through the records. So that's where Willie Nelson had ended up. She rescued him from female vocalists, stopping long enough to read the lyrics to one of his older songs. "I always get that one wrong," she muttered.

Before long, the albums were scattered around her. She lay flat on her stomach, her head resting on her folded arms. She had allowed plenty of time, and she was suddenly so tired. Simon and Garfunkel had a way of doing that to her. She closed her eyes as a madrigal harpsichord lulled her into gently distorted dreams of scarlet battalions and herbs.

She must have been asleep for over an hour, when she shifted her weight, wiggling her toes to discourage the fly that had lighted on her foot. Yellow rays of morning sunshine filled the room. Simon and Garfunkel had long since ceased to tantalize her with hazy dreams. She rolled to her back and covered her face with her forearm, stretched, yawned, then curled onto her side.

She was halfway between sleep and awareness, fading deeper into dreams, when the fly landed on her thigh. Before she could rouse herself enough to brush it away it was gone again, then was back again, licking the tender skin behind her knee.

"What," she rasped, flipping over and straight into Jeff's arms. Chagrin flooded her as he settled in beside her on the floor. What time was it?

"Go back to sleep," he said firmly, using two fingers to close her eyes, even as his other hand slithered under her blouse. "You don't talk back that way."

"The hell you say." She moved to bat his hand away from her body, but suddenly pulled it closer to her as his fingers danced lightly over the underside of her breast.

"Where...where did you come from?" she asked grog-gily, arching against the floor as he molded her with his palm. "I...I don't remember sending out for this."

"I've been lurking in the ivy, waiting for some unsus-pecting virgin to leave her window open so I could slip in and have my way with her." He let his free hand slide down her bare thigh, then back up again. "The virgins in this neighborhood are a cautious lot, I'm afraid. I had to settle for the loose woman—"

"Brazen hussy," she corrected on a sigh as his fingers skimmed and teased and tormented.

"Brazen hussy who left her front door unlocked. Again." His voice was stern, but his actions weren't as he nuzzled her neck, and she tilted her head back to give him more room. "I'm determined to break you of that habit."

"This...is...not...the way to...do it," she finished in a rush as his fingers worked their way under her shorts, her bikinis, and stroked the full, rounded flesh of her bottom. "Oh..."

"My," he finished for her.

"We're on the floor," she whispered hoarsely.

"Mm-hmm." Her blouse having somehow gotten worked up around her neck, his lips had found something other than speech to occupy them.

"Jeff," she groaned, "you're getting very unpredict-able. Very untrustworthy."

His lips worked magic on her breasts. Each moist tug seemed to pull something deep inside her, tightening into an ache between her thighs, until she broke away long enough to peel her blouse over her head, then melt back into his arms.

"Not at all." He raised his face to hers and grinned. "I locked the door."

A giggle started low in the back of her throat and grew. "I can't believe this."

"Believe what?"

"Believe that... Oh, goodness." She felt her cheeks flaming. "All those years ago, I had this fantasy. You were so solemn, so studious, so stuck up—"

"I was not!"

"You were!" She laughed at his consternation. "You were! I just knew you were waiting for someone to— Oh, I know it sounds dippy, but I was fourteen years old, for pete's sake. I thought you were waiting for someone to teach you how to laugh. To light up your life. To be your sunshine. And I was determined to get the job."

"An understatement if ever I've heard one," he growled playfully, drawing circles on her abdomen.

"Who would have ever thought—" she felt a gentle smile curling her lips "—that all these years later you do that for me? Make me laugh, remind me to loosen up once in a while."

"Who would have thought?" His hand stilled on her stomach, his eyes darkening. "Cecilia, I want to do more for you. So much more."

She touched his lips, traced them with her fingertip. "It's enough, Jeff, it's more than enough."

"Not for me," he said. He wove his fingers into her hair and pulled her closer, until her face was inches from his own.

She couldn't breathe.

"Cecilia, I love you."

Her eyes closed; she almost swayed at the sound of his words. A tremor of dread and anticipation swept through her. *I love you.* Words she'd never dared hope to hear from him. Words he wouldn't speak lightly, for he did nothing lightly. *I love you.* He was waiting for her to respond, but the words he wanted to hear were trapped inside. She spoke the only commitment she could make, the only words she could say. "Kiss me . . . love me. . . ."

His arms circled her bare waist. He began nibbling her shoulder, sliding kisses up her neck. Then his hands moved to skim over her ribs to cup her breasts, his fingers long and strong and dark against her pale ivory skin.

Her arms fell limp to her sides as he suckled her right breast, then her left, then her right again, each time greedier, more demanding. Every nerve twisted and ached, wanting to give into that greed, those demands. Her hands trembled as she unbuttoned the waistband of her shorts and slid them slowly to the floor. His hands tugged the thin,

silky fabric of her bikinis, slid them down her legs. Reflexively she lifted her foot to kick them off. That movement,
slight as it was, provided him the opportunity he was seeking as one hand encircled her and held her still and the other
explored the juncture of her thighs with studied precision.
He knew what he was doing. Gracious, he knew what he was
doing. He was relentless, stroking her moist heat until she
turned her face into her own shoulder to muffle the whimper and trap it in her throat as she felt herself swelling toward release. But then his hands were gone and it was a
sound of agony she stifled, not completion.

His lips closed over hers, savage and demanding. Her
mouth opened, drawing him in, meeting him with equal demand, equal frustration. She took great gulping breaths of
him, soaked the feel of him into her pores, the sound of his
harsh breathing and pounding heartbeat, the taste of desire
and passion.

"Jeff," she whispered hoarsely, pulling him to the bedroom, to the bed. He stripped off his shirt; she fumbled with
his trousers. The zipper snagged halfway down, and before
he could carefully, sensibly fix it, she'd slipped her hand
beneath the waistband of his shorts and lower, until her
fingertips found him. A choking sound came from his
throat and he fell over her. The old iron bed frame squeaked
under them as he braced himself above her on outstretched
arms while she stroked and explored. He was trembling; she
could sense him about to pull away, and instead she withdrew her hand and stroked the flat, hard muscles of his
belly. She had let him love her. She had taken and taken and
taken. This time she wanted to give.

"Lie down," she said, and he collapsed beside her, attempting to pull her with him, but she sat up, instead.
"Shhh..." She straddled his thighs, her fingers patiently
unsticking the zipper, as they'd done so many times before.
He stroked her hair, her shoulders, his fingers rigid. When
finally the zipper slid down, he raised his hips and she
tugged off his trousers, working them down his legs until
they landed in a heap on the floor. And then she reversed
her path, stroking his legs, his thighs, with teasing fingertips and with moist kisses. Slowly she eased back up to him,

over him, until her fingertips grazed the hem of his shorts. His iron-hard thighs flexed at her touch as she slid a hand under the soft, cool fabric and found the hard distended heat that awaited her.

"No," he said as he realized her intention, but she didn't listen, refused to give herself a chance to change her mind. She found the opening of his shorts and freed him, kissed him tentatively, felt him shudder, and gave herself over to the innate expertise born not of experience, but of the desire to give pleasure for pleasure. Remembering his loving, she held back nothing, even when his fingers twisted in her hair.

Then he was pushing her away from him, groaning, grabbing her by the shoulders and rolling with her, pressing her against the mattress as he eased slowly into her, holding back, even as he moved within her, relentlessly bringing her with him to the brink of completion. Her hands ran down the taut, bunching planes of his back to the small of his spine, riding his hips as they plunged, then withdrew, and plunged again. She clutched him, exploding with him in a radiating pleasure that spiraled through her to the outermost tingling reaches of her body. She thrust against him until her body had nothing left to give, accepting his driving passion until it was almost a pain. And still he moved and still she clasped, until nothing remained but the tears welling in her eyes, the heartache welling in her soul.

He didn't roll away. He stayed over her, wrapping her in his arms and rocking slowly, gently, sorrowfully, dragging the act beyond its natural bounds, and she let him, sucking her cheeks in to keep from losing it all together. She wouldn't break down. She wouldn't cry in his arms. And, heaven help her, she wouldn't explain, couldn't explain, that what he gave her was so momentous, so devastating, she was left without hope of ever loving or being loved again.

Love. Cruel word. Too easily spoken, too easily used and abused, even by the innocent man who rained it on her without thought of how barren she would be without it. She rolled her head away.

I can't, she said silently. I can't keep pretending you're the whole world until you've eaten a hole so big in me it will never be filled again.

But she didn't speak the words. Instead she whispered his name, over and over again, until his lips silenced her. They were meshed, legs and arms and bodies and souls.

They drifted into a restless sleep, and as usual, she was the first to waken. She covered them both with the quilt, then lay there in the silence, drinking in his presence. She watched the gentle rise and fall of his chest. She remembered the forever kiss, a kiss to remember forever. What was happening now had a forever feel. But this time it wasn't exhilarating and filled with the lure of more. This time she felt a frightening finality permeating her with cold. *Why?* she wanted to ask him. *Why couldn't you leave it alone? Why couldn't you leave things the way they were?*

His eyelids opened slowly, but his eyes were clear, as if he'd been awake...and waiting...and thinking...and feeling her watching him. "Cecilia."

She reached to touch his lips to trace their shape, to remember.

His words were measured. "Cecil, marry me."

She tried to pull away from him, but he wouldn't let go. "Jeff, you know it would never work. Let's just forget it."

He pulled her closer, tasted her lips, took them in a gentling kiss. "Feel that?" he murmured. "Do you feel it? I'll do whatever I have to, but you've got to believe me when I say I love you. I don't want to live without you anymore."

"You just think you want to marry me. But what about next week? What about next year? I mean, you've got to live with us for—" she choked on the words "—for the rest of our days."

"How can I convince you?" he asked, his thumbs rubbing her shoulders.

"Just slow down a minute, please," she begged. "Jeff, listen to me. We've got to be reasonable. I can't even picture you and Peter under the same roof."

"Peter's a spoiled brat." His blunt words were softened with a crooked smile. "So am I. And we're both used to getting our own way. We'll both have to give, to learn to

share you. It won't be easy, but it'll work. I know it can."
He took her hands and squeezed them reassuringly. "And
Brad and Annie are so much like you, how could I not love
them?"

"You're oversimplifying the problems," Cecilia muttered.

Jeff tugged at her chin until she couldn't ignore the pain
in his eyes. "Cecilia, do you realize how difficult this is for
me? I feel like I'm stepping blindfolded off a gangplank,
hoping the water's deep enough that I won't break my neck,
and hoping that the sharks that are circling aren't hungry,
and hoping that I can swim with my feet and hands bound—
and not giving a damn if all those hopes fall through, because the bottom line is that you're waiting under that
gangplank for me, and you're worth all the risks. I don't
have all the answers, but I know the answer starts with you
and me. Together. Whatever else it takes, I'm willing."

"Jeff, I want to believe you so badly."

"Sweet, sweet Cecil." The kiss he offered her was almost
reverent, beseeching, his lips soft against hers, continuing
the promise his words had begun. "Give me a chance," he
whispered. "Give us a chance."

"No," she answered, tears welling in her eyes.

"Tell me why." He rose up beside her. "What do I have
to do? " he demanded. "What do I have to say that I
haven't said? What do I have to promise that I haven't
promised? For God's sake, Cecilia, tell me, once and for all
what I'm doing wrong?"

"Wrong? You're not doing anything wrong, you're just
you."

"What the hell are you talking about?" He released her
hands.

"You, damn it! You! You're—you're so perfect!" She
tossed her head angrily. "I didn't want this! I knew it would
never work. I told you to stay away, didn't I? I managed fine
on my own until you came along. I told you that in the beginning, didn't I? You're trying to force me, to force yourself, into disaster."

"I didn't force anyone or anything!" He rolled away from
her, the tension palpable between them. His movements

were jerky with barely controlled frustration as he tugged on his shorts, his trousers, then, bare chested, leaned against the old dresser and faced her.

"I fought like hell against coming here, against coming to you from the very beginning. You think this was easy for me? I don't play games, not that kind! And I'm tired of having you brand me with some kind of weird idea of perfection! I wasn't perfect when I was eighteen, and maybe that's what terrified me so much. I didn't want anybody getting close enough to find out how imperfect I was, and you were the one who kept pushing, pushing— Well, I'm sure as hell not perfect now!"

"But you're obsessed with trying to be!" she said, wiping tears with the backs of her hands. "You don't screw up your bank book and you don't drop your towels on the floor and you—"

"Oh, grow up." He paced away from her. "What's the real reason you don't want to marry me?"

His anger hung between them and she shivered, not because she felt cold, but because she knew the chilling answer. He snatched the quilt from the floor and tossed it at her. She wrapped it around her shoulders and swallowed. Finally she faced him, tears streaming down her face.

"You want to know what I'm afraid of? I'll tell you what I'm afraid of! I'm terrified of needing you. Because I don't know if I've got what it takes to pick up the pieces if I ever let myself get close to someone again and it doesn't work."

"That's it?" he asked, his voice strangled.

She nodded mutely.

"Do you realize what you're saying? This—" his hands sliced the air "—this steel wall I'm banging against—it's not even the issue! The children aren't the problem at all." His tone was low, controlled, but his anger was as evident as if he had shouted. "The problem is that you're scared of *needing* me?"

Moments passed and finally he added, his voice hoarse, "I thought there wasn't anything we couldn't work out. The kids, our differences. You see, Cecilia, I've spent the past weeks hoping, praying and finally believing that you needed me, loved me, would want me to be in your life. You're such a damn good mother, always putting your kids first, and I understand that. But that's not the way it was at all, was it? The kids were your excuse, your shield."

"No," she whispered. And then she added, more painfully, more honestly, "Maybe."

"Now let me get this straight. If your kids adored me—if I were a damned scoutmaster, for God's sake—you'd still say no?"

"You . . . you're not being fair."

"If you can't say yes, that's the bottom line, isn't it?" She saw the shadows shift as he moved, but not toward her. "Cecilia, don't worry. You're safe. You don't need me. I've seen that from the beginning. I tried to make a place for myself, and maybe I could have if I'd been more patient, if I'd been willing to settle for less. But I'm just too selfish for that. I'm tired of being the something extra in your life."

She heard the front door hinges squeak, long and grating, the screen shut, muffled and final. She stumbled to her feet, to the foyer, wanting to call him back, yet knowing it was over. When she heard his car drive away, she fell against the door, her trembling hands covering her face, the quilt sliding to the floor.

Eleven

Cecilia could almost mark off, hour by hour, her existence during the ten days since Jeff had left her.

At first she'd felt only numb acceptance. She couldn't marry him. He couldn't stay in her life on her terms. She hadn't expected him to. The house wrapped its familiar, comforting arms around her. She played the music that had masked the empty, painful places in her life after the divorce. She slept. It had been years since she'd slept that dead-to-the-world kind of sleep that sucked her under and blocked out the pain.

The kids had returned, too, full of their adventures at the Alamo and Sea World, and they noticed when her enthusiasm was too forced and too quickly spent. Monday afternoon had been hell. The kids had their playoff tickets and, of course, expected to go to the Mavericks game. Not knowing what else to do, she'd taken them...to be haunted by the empty seat where Jeff should have been. She had muttered an explanation—Jeff obviously hadn't gotten back from his "business trip" in time to attend—and in the frenzy of the loudest arena in the National Basketball Association, no one questioned her excuse, not even Peter.

And when they asked why she wasn't yelling, cheering, jumping up and down as the Mavs came from behind and won by thirteen, she had the best excuse of all. My voice. I can't strain my voice. I have to sing tomorrow.

Tonight, Wednesday, had been the same. Walking up the steep concrete steps at Reunion Arena, she'd scanned their row, looking for that familiar head of brown hair and the tall, lanky frame...and found the empty chair. She was numb, too numb to care, she told herself. Liar, she called herself. She cared. God, she cared.

The children had fallen into an exhausted sleep on the way home from the game and had been in their beds for hours. She would have to explain, somehow, why Jeff wouldn't be around anymore. But not now. Not when she couldn't even talk about Jeff without her throat tightening and her heart aching.

But she was right, damn it. She might be miserable, but that didn't change the fact that she was right.

She stared into the darkness, the heavy scent of lemon oil from her cleaning spree still clinging to the air. She should be very proud of herself. Her life was continuing, smooth as clockwork. Smoother than usual. Recordings, basketball games, soccer practice—she was too busy to fret.

See? she said to the man who wasn't there to hear. Without you, I can manage better than with you. I'm fine now. It was nice, Jefferson, but all good things come to an end. Ours was a little better than usual, and ended a littler harder than usual, but good ol' Cecil always bounces back.

"Mom?" Peter's voice was low, urgent.

Her head throbbed with fatigue as she turned to him. His thin form was silhouetted in the doorway.

"Have you been sitting in here all night?"

All night? She repeated to herself, finally noticing the pink-gold tinge peaking through the lace draperies at the window.

"Are you sick?" He stood beside her.

"I'm fine," she said. "I just couldn't sleep."

"But all night?"

She pulled him close. "No," she lied. "I woke up early and decided to watch the sunrise. Are you hungry? How about breakfast?"

"Pancakes?"

"Okay, sure. Why not?"

They walked together toward the kitchen, but then he stopped her. "Mom?"

"What?"

"I love you."

A light blinked on his telephone. Jeff raised his head from his arms and picked up the receiver.

"Jeff, er...you have a visitor. A Mr. Evans."

"Wait two minutes, then send him in," Jeff directed, bemused. He straightened his collar and shrugged on his suit jacket. What was Robert Evans doing at his office? A prickle of unease crawled up his neck.

When he saw the "Mr. Evans" who entered, he sprang to his feet. "Peter? Well...well, how are you? Come in and sit down." He fumbled over the words, and was irritated with himself for doing so.

Peter sat across the desk from Jeff and trained his cool blue-gray eyes on the usurper of his mother's affections as calmly as if he were the adult with the upper hand. His hair was perfectly combed; even his cowlick was flat. Jeff recognized the scent of Cecilia's mousse with a pang of longing.

"Is your mother with you?"

Peter shifted in the chair. "No. I rode the bus. I had to transfer three times."

"What are you doing on this side of town?"

Peter fixed Jeff with a penetrating stare. "I think we need to talk."

Isn't that supposed to be my line? Jeff thought, narrowing his eyes. He was suddenly a little warm, which he preferred to blame on his jacket.

Peter scanned the gray and burgundy graphics on the wall. "You have a nice office."

"Thank you."

"You must be pretty well off."

Jeff felt an eyebrow arch, and tried hard not to show his surprise. Maybe the kid wanted a loan?

"I mean, you're successful."

Jeff decided it was safe to agree. He nodded.

"My mother respects your opinions."

Jeff swallowed hard. The kid must not know about their breakup. She must be cool if she could pull that off.

The boy's chin raised, and for a second Jeff saw a flash of Cecilia in that stubborn chin, those rebellious eyes. He threw his thin shoulders back. "I need your help."

"I . . . I beg your pardon? Peter? Is something wrong?"

The boy shrugged. "Sort of."

A light flashed and a buzzer blared on Jeff's desk. "Damn." He picked up the phone. "Can this wait?"

"Well . . . sure."

"I'm leaving now." Jeff hung up, his mind racing. What on earth was the kid doing, asking him for help? "Come on, let's get out of here so we won't be interrupted."

As Peter followed him silently as they left the office, Jeff was aware of the stares following them. In the parking garage he finally broke the strained silence. "Peter," he began as they climbed into the car. "I'll help you however I can."

Peter fastened the seat belt. "My father wants me to come live with him and Monica."

Jeff gripped the steering wheel, his gut twisting. Two weeks ago he would have believed that such an arrangement would solve his biggest problem. Now he thought how much the separation would hurt Cecil. "Do you want to live with them?" he asked, starting the car.

"I don't know. Dad never wanted me to stay in public school, and he and Monica are talking about moving closer to some prep school that's supposed to be pretty neat."

"Oh, really?" Jeff gripped the steering wheel even more tightly as he pulled onto Turtle Creek Boulevard.

"The house they're looking at has a special study for me. Dad says he'd fix it up with some old Digitox equipment from his office. Dad says he's afraid I won't reach my full potential if I stay with Mom."

Son of a bitch. Jeff gunned the accelerator, throwing Peter back against the seat as a light turned green. He took a slow breath and forced himself to measure his words. "How do you think I can help you?"

"You could tell Mom you think it's a good idea."

Sure he could. And destroy any chance he ever had of marrying Cecilia. "It doesn't make any difference what I think, and I wouldn't presume to offer an opinion," Jeff said. "This is between your mother and father, and frankly, I'm appalled that your father has brought you into the middle of it this way."

"It was my idea."

Jeff stared at him, stunned. So the little brat was that calculating, moving in with Robert and the ice goddess because they offered the best perks. He had never felt such anger toward a child. This was going to kill Cecilia. And Peter wanted Jeff to be the heavy. "I see," he hissed, straining to concentrate on his driving. After another block he gave up and pulled over to the curb.

"I don't want to hurt my mother," Peter said desperately. "I know how she feels about you, and if you—if you let her know—if you—" His words stumbled to a stop, his cheeks flaming with embarrassment.

"If I what?" Jeff prodded, his anger difficult to conceal.

"Are you going to marry my mother?"

How many bombshells could the boy drop in the span of ten minutes? "I don't know," he replied.

"Who are you trying to kid?" Peter released the seat belt and grabbed the door handle. "You're over all the time," he said, not meeting Jeff's eyes, "and she spends every weekend with you that we're away."

"What makes you think—"

"Good grief, I'm not stupid," Peter shot back, twisting in the seat to face him. "She's crazy about you. So I want to know, are you gonna marry her?" When Jeff remained silent, hope flickered in the depths of the boy's eyes. "Or did you dump her?"

"I didn't dump her," Jeff snapped. God, the arrogance of the kid!

The boy's shoulders slumped a bit. "If you really care what happens to my mother," he said with determination, "you'll help me. You'll help me make it so it won't hurt her," he pleaded.

"How?"

"I don't know how!" Peter said, his voice cracking. "You're the one who knows how to make her happy, not me!"

There was no disguising the tremble in the boy's chin. Jeff felt something tighten reflexively inside of him, a tight hard core of pain, of pity. He knew how hard it was to hold back those tears, and for the briefest moment he found himself responding to the boy's dilemma. Sure, Cecilia was going to be devastated, but what about Peter? If he really wanted to live with his father... But he had never said that, had he?

Jeff pretended to adjust the leather cover on the steering wheel while the boy visibly fought for control. He knew better than to humiliate the kid with sympathy. His hands stilled, and he found himself staring at the boy in shock. He knew... he felt pain and pity, because looking at those stiff shoulders, those cool, arrogant eyes, that face now rigidly set and controlled again, the truth slammed through him.

He had been a boy like Peter.

And in realizing that, he knew that the kid's words probably had little bearing on what he was actually feeling—except when Peter had said he didn't want to hurt his mother. That, Jeff believed.

And to what extremes would he go to keep from hurting his mother? Jeff finally realized why Peter had come to him. Peter would do anything for his mother. Even leave her and convince her it was his own preference, if he thought she would be happier with Jeff.

You're the one who knows how to make her happy.

If Peter only knew the truth.

"Well, are you going to help me or not?"

Suddenly the boy's arrogance wasn't as galling, as abrasive. Jeff found himself laughing a little, even though it hurt. Takes one to know one. Sure it does. Which was exactly why he and the kid had hit it off wrong from the start. They had each other's number.

Stay away from my mother.

Get out of my way, kid, I'm coming through.

This town ain't big enough for the both of us.

Jeff started the car. "I'm going to help you," he said.

Relief mixed with panic swept over the boy's face. "How?"

"Don't say anything to her about this conversation," Jeff said, avoiding his question.

"Don't worry." Peter's tone was entirely too bitter for a ten-year-old child, but Jeff remembered about bitterness, too. How well he remembered sneering to hide the soft spots, acting superior to hide the gaping holes in his ego.

"I've got to have time to think about the best way to handle this." Jeff suddenly felt drained—and stupid. Incredibly stupid to have missed the truth from the beginning. He couldn't stand the kid because the kid was too much like him, too piercing a reminder of his own faults. For a time Jeff drove in silence, then in spite of himself asked, "You . . . you really dislike me, don't you?"

Peter studied him for a moment, caught off guard. "I don't know why," he said slowly. "But I do."

Jeff understood Peter's frankness, as well. Honesty, no matter how difficult, was always the best policy. "I think I could grow to like you, Peter, despite us both."

"Sure you could," Peter mocked scornfully. "You just want my mother, free and clear. It's too bad Monica can't stand Brad and Annie, isn't it? Then you'd really have Mom where you want her."

"That's not true," Jeff said softly. He glanced at the boy's sharp profile and felt his throat tighten. The tough kids who fight affection the hardest are the ones who need it the most.

Jeff knew better than anyone that Peter didn't need a private school nearly as much as he needed the spontaneous hugs of his mother and the blind adoration of his brother and sister. Robert was worried that Peter wouldn't develop to his full potential as a great mathematician or scientist. But Cecilia was the one who saw his potential as a great kid. "I'd better get you home."

Jeff parked in front of the house, fully prepared to meet a barrage of questions. He and Peter were starting up the walk, when the front door slammed open and Cecilia ran out, her purse and keys in her hand.

"Thank God!" She grabbed Peter and gave him a quick hug. She didn't seem surprised to see Jeff with him; she was obviously distracted, upset. "It's Brad. His coach called. There were some broken bottles on the practice field, and they didn't know it until he—he slid into one. It's—it's his leg. They're waiting for me at the hospital—" She spun and grabbed Peter by the shoulders. "Watch Anne-Elizabeth for me. I tried to call Carol, and she's not home, but maybe she'll be back soon. I—I just don't know what else to do."

"I'll stay," Jeff said quickly.

"I can handle it," Peter snapped. "Go on, Mom. I'll watch her."

"I'll stay," Jeff repeated more firmly. "Unless you want us to go with you."

"Oh, no. Just stitches, his coach said. He said it's just a—a lot of blood. Annie would—she'd be upset."

Peter shook his head and rolled his eyes. "She'd love it. I say we go."

"No." Cecilia took Peter's chin in her hand. "I'm going by myself." She raised her gaze to Jeff and his stomach lurched.

The shadows under her eyes were as dark as bruises. For a moment he forgot Brad, forgot the urgency that demanded she leave. Damn, he loved her.

"You're sure you don't mind?" she said to him over Peter's shoulder.

He wanted to take her in his arms and try to absorb her pain. "I'm staying."

"Thank you." She let go of Peter's chin and he jerked away from her, his anger and hurt palpable in the evening air. "Its an awful imposition," she began, then broke off. "I have to go. I'm sorry. Thank you."

"Lock the doors," he called as she pulled away too fast. Not that he blamed her. His heart went with her. When he finally entered the house, Peter was nowhere in sight.

He walked slowly down the hallway. "Hey, where's everybody?" he called out.

A giggle escaped from under the breakfast table.

"I happen to be a very good seeker," he said.

Another giggle. Relieved to at least have a handle on the situation, Jeff made an elaborate search of the room, looking in cabinets, the refrigerator, even the aspirin drawer, before finally sinking into a chair in mock defeat. "I guess you're too good for me," he said, sighing. A bombardment of popcorn exploded at him from under the table. "What in—"

Anne-Elizabeth crawled out with an empty bag of popcorn in her hand.

"Oh!" he said in exaggerated surprise, "I thought you'd disappeared like magic."

"Anne-Elizabeth, pick that popcorn up," Peter demanded from the doorway. "What kind of baby-sitter are you anyway?"

"The worst kind." Jeff smiled, but only to temper the edge in his voice.

"I'm sure," Peter agreed glaring.

"Okay. How about this? Why don't you go watch cartoons?"

"Kid stuff," Peter sneered.

"Or climb a tree?"

"Get real. Come on, Anne-Elizabeth. Leave the jerk alone." Peter grabbed his sister's hand. "We're going outside."

Anne-Elizabeth turned her limpid gaze from Peter to Jeff, uncertainly. "Did you bwing a su'pwize?" she asked Jeff.

Jeff remembered the half can of hot, flat root beer in the car, but dismissed it. "No. I forgot. Next time, though. I promise."

Anne-Elizabeth's disappointment was evident, and clutching Peter's hand, she asked Jeff solemnly, "Did you know you're a jerk?"

"So I've been told," Jeff answered with equal solmenity as Peter dragged her through the back door.

Then he heard a soft thumping and saw Ralph's tail wagging against the floor. "Got your head under the chair again?" The tail wagged faster. "Considering what goes on in this house, I don't blame you. But you're safe now. I'm not the one who bites."

He grabbed a banana and walked out on the back porch, Ralph ambling beside him. Spying the kids beside the doghouse under one of the pecan trees, he waved. Anne-Elizabeth waved back, but Peter ignored him and called to Ralph. Jeff shrugged and went back into the house.

The house felt strange to him. No toys were strewn in his path. Cecil's music wasn't blaring. He found it difficult to breathe. God, he loved her. He wanted her. He needed her. And just being here wrenched him with a pain he couldn't bear. He'd change her mind. He'd agree to her terms. He'd do anything, just to have her back.

And having made that resolution, he found the air came a little easier into his lungs. He wanted her to need him, and she did. There was no purpose in groveling in it. She didn't even have to admit it herself. He knew. Wasn't that enough?

The singing in his veins told him it was.

He glanced around this hodgepodge house that was hers, and the assurance that he could tolerate, hell, maybe even enjoy it, nestled more firmly in him.

He thought of Brad, his leg, Cecilia's agony, and paced nervously. The smaller the injury, the more likely they'd spend a long time in a cold waiting room while more serious emergencies were seen. He wished they'd come home. He wanted to tell her what a fool he was, to take her time, to feel right about everything. Because suddenly his assurance was so strong, he found he had the patience to wait. She'd come around. She had to.

He sank into her easy chair, trying to adjust his body to the soft contours that had molded themselves to her shape. He propped his feet on the ottoman tentatively, finding he fit better than he would have thought. This was a nice place to spend a quiet moment. Surely there were quiet moments, even with the heathens around.

Suddenly it occurred to him that the kids had been unusually quiet. He rose abruptly and headed for the back door, only to catch a sharp blow in the forehead when the heavy door swung into him. Before he could react, Peter's pale face appeared around the edge of the door.

"Hurry up! You've got to come quick before she falls. I told her to come back down, but she kept going higher."

Jeff dashed out of the house then stopped short. His gaze was drawn to the splash of purple, the tiny mop of red hair. Anne-Elizabeth was wedged high in the uppermost branches of the tree, and she was crying.

"How did she get up there?" he demanded.

"She—she must have climbed on top of the dog house to reach the branches." Peter's voice broke off in a sob. "That's the way Brad and I do it."

But Jeff was no longer listening. He reached up and grabbed a limb, hoisting himself up. "It's okay, angel," he called out soothingly, fighting to keep the fear out of his voice. "Just be real still. I'm coming up to get you." But even as he spoke the words, he felt his panic rising. She was up high in the tree where he knew the branches would be too thin to support his weight.

"Hold on," he called, working his way higher, testing each branch before settling his weight on it. As he climbed, he fought to keep from looking down. Tree climbing had never been his forte. A branch groaned under his foot. He caught the trunk and held on desperately, staring at the little girl who was still very much out of his reach.

"You must be one heck of a climber," he called.

Wide-eyed, she gripped the thin branches.

"Okay, Annie, you're going to have to be a real trooper," he began, groping for the words that would bring her to him. "Do you see that big branch by your left foot?"

"Which...one is weft?" she asked weakly.

"The one with Big Bird on it!" Peter shouted from the ground.

"Oh, great," Jeff groaned. "Annie, is a picture of Big Bird on one of your shoes?"

She nodded.

"What's on the other one?"

"C-Cookie Monster."

"Now listen to me," Jeff tried again. "There's a big limb by your left foot. The foot with Big Bird on it. Do you see it?"

Anne-Elizabeth stretched her neck and looked. "It's not big. It's wittle."

"Well, it's not really big," Jeff agreed, "but it's big enough." Doubt filled the little girls' eyes. "I want you to try to put your foot on that branch."

Anne-Elizabeth extended the toe of her shoe toward the branch. "It's too far."

"No, it's not," Jeff urged gently. "You've got long legs. You can reach it." His heart was in his throat as he watched her leg stretch again and finally settle onto the limb. She looked down expectantly at him.

"Great," he praised her. "Now I know you're a strong kid, so this next part is easy. I want you to hold on to that top branch real tight." Somewhere in the back reaches of his mind, he heard his grandfather's admonition about climbing trees. He only hoped Anne-Elizabeth was a quicker learner than he'd been.

"The most important part of tree climbing is your hands," he lectured quietly, as though their situation were a simple learning experience. "As long as you hold on tight and don't let go, you won't fall, even if your feet slip. Do you understand that?"

"I don't know if my hands are that stwong," Anne-Elizabeth said from her lofty perch.

"Sure, they are," Jeff countered with forced enthusiasm. "You can do it. Now hold on tight and *slowly* swing your right leg—"

"Cookie Monster?" Anne-Elizabeth asked desperately.

"That's right. Swing it around until both your feet are on that branch." He held his breath as she bravely did as he'd instructed. "Now I want you to ease your way over to the middle of the tree—the trunk. That's the way. Hold on . . . easy now. That's great. Just rest a minute and catch your breath."

He continued to talk her down, inch by inch, branch by branch, until she was within reach. When she finally came readily into his arms, he pressed her small body between his own and the tree trunk. His heart pounded, sweat poured off his forehead in sheer relief. Anne-Elizabeth hugged him, whimpered against him, and their heartbeats combined in a frantic rhythm.

Gramps, he implored silently, you're the expert. What comes next? But try as he might, he couldn't remember how his gramps had gotten him out of that oak tree. He could only remember the nightmares. Falling...falling... waking up in a cold sweat.

Anne-Elizabeth snuggled closer, calmer now. "I scwaped my elbow, but it doesn't hurt...much."

"You're a brave girl," Jeff said, pressing his lips into her soft curls. "And strong. After we get down, why don't we...why don't we get a pizza?"

"Peppewoni?"

So much for fear.

"Good. Now do you think you could put your arms around my neck?" Her short arms encircled his neck confidently, and he felt a quiver of emotion when she smiled at him. "Now hold on tight, and whatever happens don't let go."

He carefully worked his way down the tree. His palms were raw and his arms ached, but he grabbed the rough bark with fierce strength.

"Be careful!" Peter called from below.

"I'm trying, I'm trying," Jeff muttered.

He strained for the next limb, found it, and felt a split-second's relief before his foot slipped. Suddenly they were dangling, the bark biting into his hands. "Hold on, angel," he said with a gasp and groped for footing. Then he heard a sickening crack. Wildly he clutched Anne-Elizabeth with one arm and thrust out the other to break their fall. Branches struck his back and arms, twigs tore at his skin, as they plummeted to the ground.

"Jeff! Jeff!"

He couldn't breathe. The pain in his chest was so intense he felt as if he were being sliced in two. He opened his eyes but couldn't see. Anne-Elizabeth, he thought frantically. He wanted to sit up, but couldn't move.

"Jeff! Wake up!"

He raised an arm and brushed against someone's wet face. Peter was crying. Rolling his head to one side, he tried to focus. "Annie?" he croaked, and heaved himself up on an elbow. His vision slowly cleared, and he could breathe more easily. "Annie..." She appeared before him, her face covered with blood. "God, no!" He grabbed her, dabbing at the blood with his torn shirttail. "Say something," he begged.

"You forgot to hold tight," Anne-Elizabeth announced calmly.

"Yeah. I sure did. Where does it hurt? Where are you cut?"

"Jeff, you're hurt." Peter tugged at his arm.

"I'm fine," Jeff answered gruffly. "But your sister—my God, where is she bleeding?"

"Jeff," Peter pleaded.

"I'm okay," Anne-Elizabeth said, stroking Jeff's cheek. "Don't cwy, Jeff. I'm okay."

His throat constricted and he could barely swallow. "It's all my fault." He cradled her against him and rocked, his shoulders shaking.

"Jeff, stop it!" Peter cried. "It wasn't your fault! It wasn't! Jeff, you're hurt—that's your blood!" He sprang to his feet, jerked his own shirt over his head and began dabbing at Jeff's forehead. "You're bleedin' all over her. That's your blood!"

Slowly Jeff released Anne-Elizabeth and raised a hand to his head. His fingertips grazed a deep gash.

"You're hurt bad. You've got to go to the hospital," Peter continued.

The words sunk in slowly. Jeff pulled his hand away and saw blood.

"You're makin' a mess," Anne-Elizabeth said. "Does it hurt?" She reached to touch his wound, but he pulled away from her.

"This is *my* blood?"

"You've got to go to the hospital," Peter insisted, trying to pull Anne-Elizabeth out of Jeff's lap. "Come on, you need stitches."

"What? Not stitches. I don't need any stitches, buddy. No stitches, and no needles." He felt queasy.

"Good grief, Jeff, don't be a wimp. You've got to do something. You're bleeding everywhere."

Jeff stood up and wobbled to the porch. He stumbled and landed on the top step, grateful to lean against a post. "Don't worry about me. I've got lots of blood. We just need to make sure your... your sister's all right."

"If I don't make you go to the doctor, Mom's gonna kill me. You can't even sit up straight."

"I just got the wind knocked out of me. I'll be all right." Jeff took a deep breath, fighting the nausea. "You think, you think she's gonna be mad at you? What about me?" He rubbed the back of his neck and groaned. "She'll never forgive me for not watching... for letting Anne-Elizabeth fall."

"That's right, Jeff." Peter was suddenly at his side, tugging on his arm. "If you don't take Annie to the hospital, and she's hurt real bad, Mom will never forgive you."

"I'm not—" Anne-Elizabeth's words turned into a mumble as Peter slapped a hand over her mouth.

"You're right." Jeff pulled himself up. "Come on, angel." He took Anne-Elizabeth's hand. "You're a big girl, aren't you? We'll just go see what a ... what a fancy hospital looks like, won't we?"

"Goody." Annie beamed.

"Wait. I'll call 911," Peter said. "You can't drive!"

"The hell I can't. I'm fine," Jeff growled. By the time Peter got to the car, Jeff was behind the wheel, with Anne-Elizabeth in his lap.

Peter climbed in and pulled his sister beside him, buckling them both into the same belt.

"Hold on to her," Jeff said. "We can't let anything happen to that kid." He started the car, drove a couple of feet, then braked. "Where are we going?"

"You're headed in the right direction. Just keep going straight until I tell you to turn." Peter pressed his shirt over Jeff's cut as they drove away.

Twelve

"Don't touch that leg." Cecilia sat on the hard, molded plastic seat in the hospital examining room, anxiously jingling her car keys as she watched Brad inspect his makeshift bandage.

"You should see it," he said, picking at the knot of the bloody T-shirt wrapping his calf. "It's real deep. Mikey thought I had a chunk gouged out, but Coach said it's just pulled open and needs stitches."

Cecilia swallowed hard and gripped her keys until they cut into her fingers and palms. It was all she could do to muster another "Don't touch it. Wait for a doctor."

"I'm tired of waitin'. If you'd just look at it, you'd see. You could patch it up at home." His voice took on a whining, pleading edge, and she pulled him close and squeezed his shoulders reassuringly.

"Then Coach would have brought you home, not here." She truly knew the extent of his fear when he didn't wriggle away.

"I'll bet Peter's mad, havin' to stay with Jeff." He laughed nervously. "I'll bet they're fightin' right this very minute. Do you think Peter called him a jerk?"

"I'm sure Peter and Jeff are getting along just fine." Cecilia dug in her purse with her free hand and found two quarters in the bottom. "Sit up, and I'll get you a drink."

"But Mom, what if they have to operate? They don't want you to eat or drink anything before an operation."

"Dr. Evans," Cecilia said with a reassuring pat, "I've never heard of administering general anesthesia for a couple of stitches. Believe me, you can have a drink."

As she walked the short distance to the canned drink machine, her stomach twisted with apprehension. Brad was right. Peter and Jeff were probably at each other's throats. She should have brought the kids with her. She should have . . .

The can dropped to the bottom of the chute with a heavy kerplunk. She dug in the bottom of her purse again, but to no avail. She had only a collection of pennies and paper clips, with a couple of nickels and one dime thrown in for variety. She licked her dry lips. Why didn't they hurry up and do something?

Retracing her steps, she heard a commotion behind her and flattened herself against the wall as a nurse and an orderly dashed past with an empty gurney and wheelchair. "That must have been some wreck. Don't look now, but we've got more victims coming in," gasped the orderly.

Cecilia ducked into the examining room with Brad, carefully averting her gaze from the "incoming wounded." The last thing in the world she wanted to see right now was more blood.

She'd already pivoted away from the door, when she heard a childish voice say, "I'm not hurt! I pwomise! I want my mama!"

It couldn't be.

"That's my sister!" Brad announced loudly, then sprang forward off the examining table.

"Brad, stop! Your leg!" She whirled to face the corridor, only to catch a glimpse of Brad disappearing through the door.

"Anne-Elizabeth! Jeff! Peter! Where are you?" he shouted. "Come on, Mom. It's all of 'em!"

Cecilia dashed into the hall. Some wreck...more accident victims coming in...dear heaven, was that gurney and wheelchair for them?

Brad limped ahead of her, sticking his head in each doorway along the way. Suddenly he shouted. "They're here!" She followed him into an examining room three doors down.

The scene before her—Jeff sitting on the edge of the examining table, Anne-Elizabeth in his lap, Peter standing beside them, and all covered with blood—barely had time to register in her numb mind.

"It's all right, honey," a young man in a lab coat said as he lifted Anne-Elizabeth out of Jeff's lap. "We're going to get your mama. We just need to—" He broke off with an oath and jerked his hand away. "She bit me!"

"Annie!" Cecilia sprang forward and scooped her daughter into her arms. "What—what's going on? Oh, God. She's bleeding!" She heaved her squirming daughter back onto the table. "Please," she gasped. "Help me. I'm her mother."

"I'm Dr. Boyce," the young man said. "We need to put her in a separate examining room, ma'am, and the boy, too, until we can determine—"

"Peter?" Cecilia said, reaching for him with one hand, even as she clutched Anne-Elizabeth with the other. "What—what happened to you? The blood—"

"Mom!" Peter grabbed her arm. "We're not hurt. Make them look at Jeff! He's the one who—"

"I'm not hurt," Jeff said, and for the first time she looked straight at him and gasped. His face was pasty white, with a deep gash running diagonally across his temple, already discoloring even as it continued to seep blood. "I'm not hurt," he repeated. He seemed to have difficulty focusing, for he looked directly at Cecilia for several moments before suddenly straightening. "Uh-oh. It's you," he said. "It's all my fault."

Peter blurted out, "It's not, either!"

Anne-Elizabeth scrambled into Jeff's lap. "It's all wight," she said, stroking his cheek. "I won't wet Mama kill you."

"What?" Cecilia gasped. She spun from one bloody child to another. "What on earth is going on here?"

Jeff muttered again, "My fault."

"Don't listen to him, Mom," Peter said quickly and loudly.

Anne-Elizabeth huddled closer to Jeff. "I cwimbed too high, and Jeff forgot to hold on."

Brad glared down at his own wound. "I'll bet y'all are gonna get stitched up before me, too."

"Stitches?" Jeff roused himself and gave his head an unsteady shake. "No stitches. No needles."

"Good grief," Peter said. "What a baby." But his face was pale, and his voice shaky as he turned to the doctor. "When he landed, he hit his head, and he—he seemed like he was knocked out for a few seconds. And he said he was sick to his stomach."

Dr. Boyce frowned and made a notation on his chart. "We'll need X-rays for him." He glanced warily at Anne-Elizabeth. "Then we need to check her out."

"She's okay," Peter said.

Anne-Elizabeth raised her arm. "My elbow hurts."

Cecilia reached for her, but Anne-Elizabeth pulled away, wrapping an arm around Jeff's neck. "He's afwaid. Don't worry," she said, snuggling against his torn shirt. "I won't wet 'em hurt you."

"I think..." Jeff said, clutching Anne-Elizabeth to his chest, "I think that..." His eyes rolled backward and the doctor lunged forward to catch him as he slumped sideways.

Cecilia reached for Annie, but the little girl clung with an iron grip. "He don't want any needles," she said from beneath her mop of fiery hair. Her green eyes narrowed and she showed her teeth. "Weave him awone!"

"Anne-Elizabeth!" Cecilia stepped into the fray and grabbed her daughter. "Let go, this instant!"

The little girl's eyes filled with tears, and her arms went limp as Cecilia pulled her away. "He caught me," she said. "He forgot to hold on to the twee, but he held on to me."

"Mrs. Evans, we'll get this all cleared up. Why don't you take your little girl into your son's examining room so she can calm down."

"That figures," Brad grumbled. "I've gotta wait. Again."

Holding her daughter close, Cecilia allowed the nurse to escort her to the door. She paused and met Peter's uncertain gaze. "Aren't you coming?" she asked.

"I...I thought I'd better stay here." He shrugged uneasily, his eyes going to Jeff and the doctor, who was peering into one of those big, brown eyes with a narrow beam of light. "He's all alone. They...they might need to know something."

"Peter, you don't have to—" Cecilia began.

"I think we can handle it, buddy," the doctor assured him.

But his mind seemed set. Peter dropped into a plastic chair beside the examining table. "You'd better check his back, too," he said to the intern. "He's kind of cut up from fallin' out of the tree."

"That's the way," Cecilia panted. "Lean on me, Jeff." She braced an arm against the wall and struggled down the hall to her bedroom. Peter whipped back the covers, and Anne-Elizabeth plumped the pillows with her small fist. "We're weady," she announced, patting the pillow into place. "You can wie down now."

"This really isn't necessary," Jeff gasped as he sank to the side of the bed. "I could have gone home."

"With nobody but that damned bird to take care of you? Grow up, Jeff."

"Don't worry," Peter said. "We'll get Toulouse and bring him over here so he won't be lonely."

"Over my dead—" Cecilia began, then cleared her throat. "We'll think of something."

Jeff reached for his shoe, but Anne-Elizabeth got there first. In moments she had the laces untied. "You've got pwetty socks," she said, rubbing the red argyles with her finger.

"Thank you," Jeff replied solemnly. He raised his eyes beseechingly to Cecilia. "If you really insist on my staying here...I think I'd better lie down."

She reached forward to help him, but he brushed her hands away. He fumbled with the buttons of his shirt then shrugged it off, exposing the white bandages that wrapped much of his upper body. When he reached for his belt buckle, she grabbed the kids by the shoulders.

"Why don't we leave Jeff alone for a while?" she said, escorting them into the hall and closing the door behind her.

"How wong is Jeff staying?" Anne-Elizabeth asked, her brow knit with concern.

"Overnight should be long enough," Cecilia said. "How would you like to sleep on the living room floor with me? That way we'll hear him if he needs something in the middle of the night."

The front door banged open and Brad entered with two small pill bottles in his hands. "I found 'em. They dropped behind the seat. I'll take Jeff his." He loped down the hall and into his mother's bedroom, only a slight limp to indicate the seven stitches holding his wound tidily closed. He emerged moments later with one pill bottle, slammed the door behind him and spun to face his mother and siblings, his freckled face wreathed in a grin. "Wow! You should see Jeff's undershorts!"

"Brad, go into the living room and get off your leg," Cecilia said quickly. "And give me your medicine."

"But they're red—"

"Who wants lemonade?" Cecilia interrupted, tucking his antibiotics into the pockets of her slacks.

"Jeff wears pwetty wed socks," Anne-Elizabeth said. "I wike wed."

"Annie, make sure Brad gets off that leg. You be the doctor, all right?"

The four-year-old immediately jumped into action, grabbed her brother's arm and dragged him toward the living room. "You have to do what I tell you 'cause I'm the doctor and I said wie down!" she ordered. Brad allowed himself to be bullied into obeying, graciously accepting the plumped pillows, afghan and stuffed bear she found necessary for his recuperation.

Cecilia grabbed a tray, a pitcher and a ladle, and began preparing the lemonade.

"Mom..."

Peter stood uneasily beside her.

"You must be wondering..."

"I think that between Jeff's repeated apologies and Anne-Elizabeth's explanations I've finally managed to piece together what happened." She smiled, handing him a glass. "It's all right, Peter. Accidents happen. It's nobody's fault, and since Jeff only needed a few stitches, I think we can chalk it up to just another day in the Evans zoo, don't you?"

"I guess so. But I figured you'd want to know why—"

"Wait. Did you hear something?" she asked, her heart suddenly thumping a little faster. "I thought I heard Jeff calling." She placed two glasses on the tray. "I'll take his lemonade. And why don't you take Brad's drink to him?"

She hurried to the bedroom, entered silently, then nudged the door shut with her hip.

"Thank you," Jeff moaned.

"For what?"

"For not crashing, banging or slamming the door."

"I left a message for Robert, and when he calls I'm going to ask him come get the kids."

Jeff's brow furrowed, and he winced, gingerly touching the bandage at his temple. "Why are you sending them away?"

"Because," she said. "you don't need them banging and slamming and crashing through the house with your head about to burst."

"Oh." He blinked at her. "You really don't have to do that. I don't mind them staying."

She placed the tray on the dresser. "Let me pull the shades."

"Please."

When the room was darkened, she faced him and sighed. "Oh, Jeff."

"I thought it was 'oh, my.'"

"I don't know what to say." She clenched her hands against the small of her back. "Well, at least now you understand."

There was a moment's silence, then he said, "I think I'm too shaken up to understand anything. Why don't you humor me with an explanation?"

Cecilia knelt beside him, bringing her face close to his. "You didn't ask for any of this. You just stepped in, as usual, Mr. Nice Guy, and the next thing you know, you're in the hospital with an almost concussion." She shook her head, her throat tightening. "We'll drive you crazy, if we don't kill you first."

"That seems to be a distinct possibility." His hand fell limply to the side of the bed. "Could I have my lemonade now?"

She jumped to her feet. "Of course." She grabbed the glass, her hand trembling. "You're going to have to sit up." She eased her arm under his shoulders to help. Without warning he caught her and pulled her against his chest as he placed the glass on the bedside table with his free hand.

"Kiss me, Cecil."

"I don't think that's a good idea," she whispered. "You shouldn't—"

"It's the least you can do."

She pressed her lips tentatively against his, felt his arm tighten around her back, and closed her eyes. How could anything so disastrous as what they were doing to each other feel so wonderful, so right? She pulled away to catch her breath, and he let her.

"Thanks," he muttered. "I needed that."

She slid out of his arms.

"Where are you going?"

"You need your rest."

"My head agrees with you." He caught her hand. "You look terrible, Cecil, and you didn't fall out of a tree. So what's your excuse?"

"I don't know what you're talking about."

"The way I hear it, you're not sleeping, you're bitchy as hell—"

"Says who?" she demanded.

"Well...some of it I've surmised." He wouldn't release her hand, even when she tugged. "I'm glad to see you're surviving so well without me."

"I am," she said, unable to stem the belligerent tone of her voice.

"Cecil...don't do this."

She blinked, then swallowed hard. "Jeff, if all this today hasn't convinced you that marrying me is a mistake—"

"It hasn't."

"Then I don't know what else to say."

"Try admitting that you need me."

She jerked her hand free. "I don't need you to survive. I've managed quite well without you."

"But?"

"Well, I...I can't very well lie about it. I'm not happy." The words sounded so inadequate, yet how could she put it any more plainly?

"Is that all?"

"That's about it." She sighed.

"So what are you going to do now that you've made this discovery?"

"I guess I'm going to have to get used to being un-happy."

"I hope you aren't serious." He tried to sit up, but she applied gentle pressure to his shoulder.

"Of course I'm serious. Jeff, you have no idea how much responsibility is involved in this business of raising kids. It's..." She felt a sob growing in her throat and fought it down. "Sometimes it's more than I can handle."

"When is the last time you admitted that?" he asked softly.

"It doesn't make any difference. It's a big job, and I love it, and I do a damn good job of it. But I can't ask any-body...not even you...to share it." She raised her eyes imploringly to his. "Don't you understand? I'm not pro-tecting the kids anymore. I'm protecting you."

"Cecil."

She blinked back tears.

"I've never felt as...cared for...as I've felt today."

"Of course," she sniffed. "That's the way they are. They were scared, and they'll do anything they can for you today, but—"

"Tomorrow Anne-Elizabeth will use my socks for doll clothes and Peter will call me a jerk."

She nodded forlornly. "That's about the extent of it."

"And I'll probably growl a little and . . . learn to hide my socks."

"And your underwear," she added.

"My under—Oh, yeah. Brad."

She nodded. "So you see—"

"I see that you don't give me credit for having enough sense to make my own decisions. You're trying to make them for me, which if I did for you, you'd wallop me."

"I think that blow to the head has knocked you silly."

"Cecil, stop making excuses and admit that you're wrong, or I'll drag you to the top of that tree and toss you out on your head and knock *you* silly."

"Let's drop the subject, okay?" She couldn't stand there and listen to him talk this way. She couldn't allow this niggling hope to flicker to life in her.

"Not until you agree to marry me." He grasped her arm and tugged her down to meet his lips.

She should pull away. She could if she tried. But the ache inside her cried out for healing. She wanted to believe him. She wanted to lose herself in his eyes, those wonderful root-beer eyes. Their lips brushed gently, testing, tasting. She didn't want to hurt him. But then his fingers were twining in the hair at the back of her head, demanding more, and she gave herself up to him. Lord, he had a way of kissing her that melted her from her tingling scalp to her tingling toes. Thoroughly, the way he did everything. When his kiss ended, she rested her head on his chest, fighting the feelings he evoked in her.

What if it all bubbled and boiled down to the fact that he was so blinded by their love that he wasn't facing their problems? What if he woke up one day and wondered what the hell he was doing living in this madhouse?

Tears slipped from beneath her closed eyelids. "Don't cry," he whispered, wiping them away. "Don't cry."

She wanted to believe him.

She lay in his arms, trying to be practical, trying to be sensible, trying to be responsible. He made it so damned hard! Suddenly she froze, pulled away and stared at him in dawning shock.

"What's wrong?" he asked.

"You're not fighting fair." She clenched her hands in her lap.

"Why?"

"Because you act like you know what you're doing. You act like you're walking into this with your eyes wide open, and they aren't. They can't be. You'll—you'll end up hating me, and the kids, and—"

"Don't you dare say that."

"Jeff, tell me honestly, what would you do with a checkbook that never balances because I forget to make deposits, and forget to record checks and...well, what would you do?"

"I would find it so damned unbearable that I would probably refuse to touch the damn thing."

"You see. It would never work."

"If you think I'm going to put myself through that kind of a wringer every month, not to mention alienating Peter by usurping his job, you've got another think coming."

"But you've been trying to get your hands on my checkbook ever since that first day!"

"I know what I said. I also know that Peter treats that checkbook like a game. He takes great pride in the fact that no matter what you do to it, he unscrambles it."

"I know that, but I never figured you'd understand."

"Cecil, I understand so much more than you think I do. In the first place, stop protecting me, if that's what you think you're doing. I've protected myself too damn well for too damn long. I need a little shaking up now and again."

"And that's what I'm good for? Shaking you up?" She didn't know whether to laugh or be angry. "And what happens when things get too shaky around here? What about when—"

"You're giving me a headache." He sighed. "Cecil, go outside on the front porch and sit and swing and argue with yourself. I don't have the energy for it. And when—'' he yawned "—when you come to the amazing conclusion that you love me too much, *need* me too much to let me get away again, come wake me up and tell me.''

He rolled away from her as though that settled everything.

"You arrogant—And what if I don't come to that amazing conclusion?''

"You will.'' His voice was muffled, but unmistakably determined.

"You—you deserve—you deserve to have a house full of chaos, you're so damned cocky! And—and—'' She glared at his back, even as she felt giddy relief flowing through her. "And stop picking up after me! I refuse to live with someone who makes me feel like a slob!''

Slowly, the bed springs squeaking, he rolled back to face her. "Did I understand you correctly?''

"It's too late to back out of it. If you're so damned determined to drive yourself crazy, then the hell with it. I can't protect you forever.'' She flung her hair out of her eyes and raised her chin. "I can't keep refusing what I want and need more than anything else in the world to save your blasted sanity if you won't cooperate.'' The door cracked open behind them. "Yes, damn it. I'll marry you.''

Anne-Elizabeth's piercing squeal split the air and her sneakers thundered away against the hardwood floor. "Brad! Peter! We're gonna mawwy the jerk!''

Jeff's skin paled three shades as he clutched his head.

"Don't say I didn't warn you.''

"Maybe...maybe carpet would help,'' he offered weakly.

Cecilia closed the door firmly, locked it and crossed to the bed. "You'll be sorry,'' she warned.

"Probably,'' he agreed as she snuggled against him. He kissed her, and for a few enchanted moments, that was all she was aware of.

"I'm afraid to trust this,'' he muttered into her neck when he finally came up for a breath.

"Trust . . . us?''

"No. Of course not.'' He kissed her again, his hand trailing up and down her side as if wanting to caress, yet being restrained. "I'm waiting for a child to burst in and interrupt us." He nipped her ear. Not hard, but enough for her to shudder. "For a soccer ball to fly by." His hand finally found a convenient spot to rest; his thumb dragged a seductive arc over the fullness of her breast. "For a set of teeth to close over my thigh."

His thigh being out of reach, Cecilia nuzzled his neck and with teeth and tongue explored the tightly corded muscles. His groan rumbled against her lips and a corresponding tremor trembled through her body. "I guess you'd better get used to it," she said, sighing.

"Oh, yeah," he agreed. "I'm definitely developing a taste for chaos."

A hesitant knock sounded at the door.

Cecilia straightened her blouse. "Come in," she called.

"I thought it was locked," Jeff said as the doorknob rattled.

"It's an old lock. Brad can pick it," she replied.

Jeff gulped, but quickly took command. "We'll get a new lock."

"Whatever you say," she said sweetly.

The door opened and three heads appeared in the doorway. Brad and Ann-Elizabeth were grinning; Peter looked worried. Cecilia's stomach lurched. They should have been more cautious. They should have prepared Peter, not hit him with the news so bluntly.

Suddenly she remembered. "Peter, what were you doing with Jeff this afternoon?"

Peter avoided her eyes, only looked at Jeff for all the world as if he were pleading for something. The softest smile curled Jeff's lips. "I think it had something to do with my intentions. And since you've agreed to make an honest man of me, I think they're strictly honorable."

Peter still stared at him. What was going on? He looked . . . scared.

"I have only one reservation," Jeff went on. "That damned bird."

"Oh, well," Cecilia rushed in. "I'm sure we can find a good home for him if—"

"Over my dead body." Jeff's tones were flat and no-nonsense. "There's room for Ralph—there's room for my bird. There's room for everybody," he said succinctly. He watched Peter, his eyes strained, pleading. "But Peter, would you keep him upstairs ... in your room?"

Brad whooped with excitement, then hollered, "We got the bird!"

Peter blinked rapidly, nodding. "You bet." If Ceclia hadn't known better, she would have sworn his eyes were shimmering with unshed tears as his relieved smile took shape. "You bet," he repeated.

"Then if everything's settled, I think I'd better get some rest," Jeff said softly, and for once in their lives, the children took the hint.

When they were alone again, Cecilia bent over Jeff and gently kissed his cheek. The events of the day seemed to have taken their toll. His gentle snore vibrated against her ear.

She smoothed the sheet snugly around him. Standing, she stared down at his socks, folded and tucked carefully into his shoes, at the dusty toe of her panty hose, peeking from beneath the bed.

Oh, Lord.

They were doomed.

But blissfully so.

*   *   *   *   *

Silhouette Classics

COMING IN APRIL...

THORNE'S WAY by Joan Hohl

When *Thorne's Way* first burst upon the romance scene in 1982, readers couldn't help but fall in love with Jonas Thorne, a man of bewildering arrogance and stunning tenderness. This book quickly became one of Silhouette's most sought-after early titles.

Now, Silhouette Classics is pleased to present the reissue of *Thorne's Way*. Even if you read this book years ago, its depth of emotion and passion will stir your heart again and again.

And that's not all!

Silhouette Special Edition

COMING IN JULY...

THORNE'S WIFE by Joan Hohl

We're pleased to announce a truly unique event at Silhouette. Jonas Thorne is back, in *Thorne's Wife*, a sequel that will sweep you off your feet! Jonas and Valerie's story continues as life—and love—reach heights never before dreamed of.

Experience both these timeless classics—one from Silhouette Classics and one from Silhouette Special Edition—as master storyteller Joan Hohl weaves two passionate, dramatic tales of everlasting love!

CL-36

Silhouette Special Edition®

NAVY BLUES
Debbie Macomber

Between the devil and the deep blue sea . . .

At Christmastime, Lieutenant Commander Steve Kyle finds his heart anchored by the past, so he vows to give his ex-wife wide berth. But Carol Kyle is quaffing milk and knitting tiny pastel blankets with a vengeance. She's determined to have a baby, and only one man will do as father-to-be—the only man she's ever loved . . . her own bullheaded ex-husband!

You met Steve and Carol in NAVY WIFE (Special Edition #494)— you'll cheer for them in NAVY BLUES (Special Edition #518). (And as a bonus for NAVY WIFE fans, newlyweds Rush and Lindy Callaghan reveal a surprise of their own. . . .)

Each book stands alone—together they're Debbie Macomber's most delightful duo to date! Don't miss

**NAVY BLUES
Available in April,
only in *Silhouette Special Edition*.
Having the "blues" was never
so much fun!**